by Thaisa Frank

Desire (1982)
A Brief History of Camouflage (1992)

THAISA
FRANK

A BRIEF
HISTORY OF
CAMOUFLAGE

BLACK SPARROW PRESS
SANTA ROSA—1993

ACKNOWLEDGMENTS

Some of these stories were previously published in *The City Lights Review, Forehead* and *Word of Mouth* Volumes 1 & 2.

I am grateful to Kelsey Street Press, who published *Desire,* for their permission to reprint "Silence" and "Snow."

Special thanks to Dorothy Wall for her extraordinary gifts of insight and friendship.

T.F.

Second Printing

LIBRARY OF CONGRESS CATALOGING-IN-PUBLICATION DATA

Frank, Thaisa
  A brief history of camouflage / Thaisa Frank.
    p.   cm.
  Stories.
  ISBN 0-87685-857-4 (cloth) : — ISBN 0-87685-856-6 (pbk.) : —
ISBN 0-87685-858-2 (signed cloth ed.) :
  I. Title.
PS3556.R3345B75   1992
813'.54—dc20   91-39923
                                                       CIP

this book is for my son
Casey Rodarmor

TABLE OF CONTENTS

I. A BRIEF HISTORY OF CAMOUFLAGE

II. NIGHT VISITS

I.
A BRIEF
HISTORY OF
CAMOUFLAGE

STORIES WE BEGAN TO TELL

A FEW MONTHS BEFORE HE SAID HE WAS MOVING OUT, my husband began to tell me bedtime stories. His habit had always been to fall asleep as soon as he got into bed, but one night, without ceremony, he began:

"Once there was a woman who was so large, her dimensions were measured in longitude and latitude instead of inches. Her measurements, or degrees, were known only to her; but once she took a lover who set about measuring her secretly in the dark. To his amazement he found out that she had the same longitude and latitude as the city of Thebes—a discovery which excited him, although he couldn't say why."

At this point he stopped, as if surprised by what he was saying. I leaned forward and said:

"What happened? Did he tell her?"

"No," he said. "He never told this to the woman, but kept on making love as if nothing had changed. For a while she seemed to notice nothing, but one night she said: 'It's the oddest thing, but whenever we make love I keep feeling like you're exploring ancient ruins.

Tell me, has anything changed?' The man could have lied, but he felt impelled not to, and so he confessed everything, and the woman ended up feeling miserable because it wasn't her he loved after all. He tried to explain that it *was* her; but she didn't believe him, and she made him leave, right in the middle of the night and they never saw each other again."

It was quiet when he finished. In the dim light his eyes looked deep and large. He took off his glasses, and sighed, as if telling the story had required tremendous effort.

"Is that the end?" I asked.

"Yes, that's the end," he said.

"How did you think that up?" I asked.

"I don't know. It just came to me."

Every night other stories followed: There was a story about a man who fell in love with a tree and set up his computer in a forest, and a story about a woman whose lover was a sheepdog she'd known as a human in a previous life. There was a story about a man whose body was illuminated and a story about a child whose mother became a dinosaur. He told me these stories in a driven, abstracted way, as if recounting information from the air. I sat next to him listening.

Much later I realized the stories were codes,

urgent messages about his own condition—but I didn't think about this at the time. At night when we got into bed, I couldn't wait for him to start; and though I'd never liked our bedroom—it was small and full of old furniture—whenever he told stories it became transformed to a crowded, intimate theater.

Since the stories were so unusual, I always asked where they came from and he always said: "I really don't know. They just came to me." My question and his answer became a ritual, an exchange that marked the story's end. But one night after an unusually complicated story, he said:

"You told me that one—remember? About a year ago, at that hotel in Bangkok when we couldn't sleep."

I remembered the hotel—a small, two storey building with filigreed bannisters, that we'd stayed at on our way back from Bali. It had no air-conditioning, not even in the lobby, and the bedroom contained an old-fashioned pitcher that smelled of mothballs.

"I never told you that story," I said. "I couldn't have. I've never heard it."

"But you did," he said. "It was that night when we opened all the windows and drank iced tea and talked about what we wanted to do to the house when we got home. We got to talking about the roof, and the plumbing system, and then you told me that story." He said this as though he meant it.

There was no way I could have told him the story. First, because I'd spent most of that night in the hotel lobby, trying to cool off before its massive, half-open door. And second, because it was completely beyond my imagination—so much so, I could hardly remember the details, and didn't even want to:

The story had been about a thirty-five-year-old man whose heart, lungs and liver, had turned into the plumbing system of an old house. The clangings and groanings kept his wife awake all night, until she put a wrench down the man's throat and turned him off. Quiet ensued and she got some sleep, but the next morning when she put the wrench down his throat to turn him back on, he was dead. Her explanation to the police was so improbable, they held her on bail until they performed an autopsy. Finally they released her, and she returned home grief-stricken—imagining she could hear groaning in the plumbing of their own house. She sold their property and moved to Florida.

While he was telling me this story, I had been feeling unbearably sad, almost to the point of asking him to stop. Every time I thought about the wife listening to this old and terrible plumbing inside her husband, it took some effort not to cry; and when she finally guessed what was happening and stuck a wrench down the man's throat, I felt a curious relief—the same I'd felt when our senile dog had died.

I knew I couldn't have told him this story; but the more he kept insisting he'd heard it from me, the more I began to think I'd told it to him after all. It was as though the truth became a path I was too exhausted to follow. I could even see myself in that hotel room, wrapped in a white bedspread, with dirty fringes, sitting on the edge of the bed, telling him about that man. The more I saw this the more I grew furious that he should tell me this story again.

"That story was for you," I said, getting on top of him and holding him by the shoulders, "and I asked you never to repeat it—not to anybody, least of all to me."

"No you didn't."

"Oh, yes I did. And even if I hadn't, I'd think you could figure it out."

The light was on, so I could look into his eyes; they were incredulous, with a certain softness, and for a moment we were brought to a delicate, almost loving tension. I even thought we might make love, but suddenly he shook me off, and said:

"I am that man and you can never deny it. His life is my life. How can you expect me not to talk about him?"

He said this in a whisper, almost like a curse, and I knew that it was true, and any more stories would have to come from me. Thrown to my side of the bed, not knowing how to begin, I waited until a story appeared—it was small and somewhat tremulous. But before I'd even taken a breath, he touched my arm and said:

"Please don't tell me that story. Please don't tell me anything."

NIGHT SOUNDS

FOR A WHILE, BEFORE MY HUSBAND LEFT ME, THE thought of leaving him assumed the magnificence and complexity of a forest. I never thought about where I would go, only that I would leave, and this thought made me feel like a stranger in my own house, which was actually half a house, because the lower half was rented to other students. At night, when Dan was in his study reading, I would wander around the house in a cool, dispassionate way, looking at rooms like an intruder. I cared less about what was in the rooms than the sense of unoccupied space—that cathedral-like sweep that houses assume at night—and I enjoyed feeling vaguely illicit. Dan was always under the impression that I was asleep, and to ensure this I didn't come out until late—part spy, part goblin, part rodent.

During my prowls, I visted every room in our house, with the exception of Dan's study, and the apartment downstairs. This apartment was dark, and its ceilings were low, giving the impression of an archives. When we'd first moved there, its occupant had been a brooding, reclusive graduate student in Germanic studies who showed me an essay about Heidegger that shocked me with its Teutonic darkness. I'd fallen a little in love with him, but then he had a nervous breakdown and moved out, leaving me to return his library books.

Now this apartment was rented to two undergraduate women who had transformed the archives into a dormitory. They'd covered the walls with banners, filled the beds with stuffed animals and misted every pore of air with hair-spray. Their names were Patti and Jayne and they were courted by shy, hulking athletes who arrived every night in separate cars. As I prowled, I often heard sighs and giggles, as well as moans of exalted love-making coming through a wall in the kitchen. I'd never been impressed with their turquoise T-shirts and brand-new cars. But the sounds were amazingly passionate and seemed to consecrate the house. The first night I heard them, I imagined them all in the same bed—a tangle of eight arms and eight legs, like Shivas; and then I imagined them in separate beds, making love only with their voices. After the sounds died down, I walked around my own house feeling even more displaced, and the next night, and the night after that, as if it were my right to listen, I ended my prowls in a corner of the kitchen. I poured a glass of wine and pulled up a chair just like I was listening to the radio.

During these times Dan was in his study. A few years later, after we split up, we met by chance on a Paris street and mistook the miracle of this meeting as a sign that we should try all over again. But in those days, as if orchestrated by separate clocks, we hardly spent time together at all. Dan's study was catty-corner to the kitchen and though its narrow window I often saw his hands, reaching for cigarettes. They were long, thin, industrious, and his study was sparse. I envied Dan's sense of order, and this added to my guilt as I listened to the kids. In response I closed my eyes.

One night Dan came into the kitchen so quietly I didn't hear him. There was only the uncanny sense of his bulk, and by the time I knew he was there, he'd seen me. Dan looked purposive and sly, as though he had meant to catch me; he also looked happier than I'd seen him in a long time.

"What in God's name are you doing?" he asked, coming over to the wall.

"Nothing, I just can't sleep," I said. I was trying to hide my sandwich and when I saw I couldn't, I ate it blatantly.

"But what were you doing next to that wall?"

"Nothing, just listening to the house."

"I don't believe you," Dan said, and he went over to the wall and pressed an ear against it. "What are you?" he said after a minute. "Some kind of voyeur?"

"No, I just happened to be sitting here."

"I'll bet," said Dan. He put his ear against the wall again and listened as if he were performing some distasteful duty. His eyes got dreamy. "Boy, they sure go at it," he said. "Do you think all four of them could be in the same bed?"

"No. It's just the acoustics."

"I'm not so sure. Listen!"

I put my ear to the wall, and a graphic image of all four of them arose in my mind. It was different listening together. Dan and I started to lean against each other and soon, without negotiating birth control, we made love on the floor, adding our own sounds quietly. Afterwards we made pillows from our clothes and settled down in the kitchen. The soft moans were still coming up from below.

"So is this what you do when I'm wrestling with Blake?"

"Only when I can't sleep. It's circumstantial."

"You're still a voyeur," Dan said—a statement, not an accusation—to which I answered, "No, I'm not," although Dan was touching a raw nerve since I'd actually gone to the library and gotten a book about voyeurism which said: *Circumstantial voyeurs do not travel or pay money for gratification, but happen upon situations only by accident.* This information had reassured me.

It felt intimate, lying together on the kitchen floor, listening to the hum of the refrigerator. Indeed, we were drifting off to sleep, when suddenly, from below, we heard a loud yell, and one of the women said—harshly—"God dammit, you *bit* me!" Then there was another voice, less audible, and the sound of something, or someone, being pounded. A door slammed, and we heard water running.

Dan and I sprang apart. In all my nights of listening, the kids had never fought, and now I felt guilty, as if our love-making had upset a delicate balance.

"Do you think we should go downstairs?" Dan said, sounding older than twenty-eight. "See what's going on? I feel protective."

"No. I think we should let them alone. It's a love-fight."

"How do you know?"

"Just a guess."

We waited, listening. There was nothing for a while, then a male voice began to sing *Hello Stranger*. Both of us felt encouraged; but when the song stopped there was dead silence.

"I'm going down there," said Dan, pulling on his jeans.

"Leave them alone. They'll know we were listening."

"No. They could get into trouble. Or wreck the house. I just can't sit here and let it happen."

In a sense he was right. Dan and I were the official caretakers of the house. We saw that the lawn was mowed, got a cut in rent for being responsible. I watched while he put on his shirt, grabbed a broom, and went outside. I heard him knocking on the door, and then there were muffled voices. After a moment, I pulled on my shirt and crept to the narrow landing above our garden, where, through the filigreed railing, I could see Patti standing outside in a white bathrobe. Dan was standing next to her.

"It's nothing," I heard her say. "We just got into this . . . hassle . . . I'm sorry." She seemed embarrassed and Dan smiled, looking avuncular.

"It's okay," he said. "We were just concerned."

Patti didn't seem reassured. Dan leaned closer.

"Don't worry," he said, in a conspiratorial voice. "Fighting is a good thing. Audrey and I don't fight enough."

"Really?" Patti seemed more polite than interested.

"Yes. Except for the other night—I'm surprised you didn't hear us . . . we got into this terrible hassle. Some things even broke."

"Really?" She showed the same strained politeness.

"Yes. I broke a plate and Audrey broke a cup.

We just threw things against the wall."

Dan's voice got low. He was telling her god-knows-what. I could see him towering above Patti, illuminated in the moonlight.

"We used to think that fighting was bad for our marriage," Dan continued, with the wisdom of a married man, "but the other night we realized it saves it. No, honestly, you learn those things over time . . ."

For a moment I felt that I was a hair's breadth away from standing up on the landing and making a scene. The feeling only lasted an instant, and then I was myself again—patient, hidden from view.

"Fighting is everything," Dan continued. "People have always fought. Think of the cave people. Those brawls in Lascaux."

He went on for a while as if a book of history had opened, an enormous book of domestic quarrels. Patti nodded energetically, especially when he spoke about the Renaissance. Finally, during a pause, she thanked him and left with an embarrassed bow. Dan stayed in the garden, leaning on his broom. He looked elliptical, calligraphic, almost sketched.

"How come you lied?" I asked, looming over the edge of the filigreed railing.

"I didn't," said Dan. "I embellished. Does it bother you?"

"You didn't embellish. You lied. I never broke a cup. And we didn't fight the other night. We haven't fought in a while."

Dan looked at the ground.

"Well did we?"

"No, we didn't. But why should it bother you if I make up something to amuse myself?"

"I don't know, but it does."

Dan stooped over, picked up a leaf from the ground. Then he said, "Well why shouldn't I make things up? You never tell me what's going on with you."

"No," I said, "I don't."

"Well I don't tell you things either."

"Like what?"

"Just a lot."

It seemed quiet in the garden. There was tension in the air, the leaves were listening.

"What is it that you don't tell me?" I said, taking· a step forward on the landing.

"Do you really want to know?"

"Yes."

"All right, then, I'll tell you: It's that sometimes I think that we don't fit. There's a Chinese saying that people who are meant to be together are like a piece of paper torn in half. That's not us."

I was sorry I'd asked. I felt exactly the same way, but right then I felt I wanted to stay with Dan forever, poised on the landing, watching him in the garden. The moon was bright, everything looked ephemeral.

"Hey listen, Dan, I love you," I said.

"Oh, I love you, too. Love has nothing to do with it."

I knew he was right, and after a moment I went inside, no longer feeling like a spy, just a woman entering her house. I didn't turn on the light, but waited, listening to Dan in the garden. Scrape. Scrape. Scrape. Scrape. I could hear him starting to sweep. And then I peered outside. There he was with his broom, sweeping stones, leaves, weeds—a calligraphic man, putting everything in order.

THE MOLE

HE NOTICED THE MOLE THE ONLY TIME THEY EVER MADE love, a light blue mole, nestled on the inside of her thigh. It was delicate, translucent, and when he touched it, it felt fragile, like a mushroom. He was an ear, nose and throat specialist, and hadn't thought about moles in many years, but later, when they were sitting on his bed talking, it occurred to him that it might be cancerous. The mole was blue, and, from medical school, he remembered that blue moles were often malignant. And so he looked at Sharon, sitting opposite him on his bed, wrapped in his shirt, her hair falling over to one side, wondering how to broach the subject. She was a medical-technician—certainly she knew about such things and surely she'd be angry if he presumed she didn't. Also he had a feeling she didn't like him very much: She was a tall restrained woman of about twenty-eight, with a sense of smoldering inner heat he'd been unable to release, even for an instant.

"This is my kid," he said, by way of entering into a certain softness with her, a softness that might allow him to mention the mole. He reached over to his bedside table and showed her a photograph of his son in his Little League outfit. "I'm divorced," he said as he handed her the picture. "My kid is eight."

"Oh," she said, lifting the picture, and looking at it without much interest. "I guess I already knew that."

═══════

After a while, she left, pausing by his collection of geodes, the only bright thing in his sparse apartment, and refusing his offer of a taxi. He was glad he hadn't mentioned the mole, but later, around midnight, he began to worry again. He had never been interested in diseases of the skin—he preferred what was hidden, accessed through apertures and tunnels—but now he pulled out his old medical school textbooks and looked at photographs of moles. None of them looked like her mole: they seemed darker, larger, less fragile. He went to bed reassured, yet the moment he woke up he remembered. The mole was dark in his memory, almost black.

═══════

"For God's sake," said a dermatologist friend, whom he'd cornered at the hospital, "she's probably had it for ages, and if she's a medical technician, she knows all about it." They were in the doctor's lounge and he'd told her the entire story. "How old did you say she was? Twenty-eight?"

"I don't know, I didn't bother to ask."

"You don't know how old she was, but you noticed her mole—Dennis, you're distraught. I bet you've been sleeping around too much." The friend laughed, and added: "It's your divorce. You should stay out of circulation for a while."

The conversation relieved him, but later that day, he went to the medical library. Moles are like hieroglyphs, he thought, walking through the stacks like a sleuth—hard to decipher, crudely beautiful. As soon as he opened the books (he did so secretly, with the sense of seeking forbidden knowledge) he felt sucked into a universe of moles. Horribly, a small purple mole on the thigh of a young woman had turned out to be fatal, but eleven black moles on the back of a middle-aged man were benign. The more he looked at the pictures, the more Sharon's mole changed shape and color in his memory.

"Did her mole have a hair on it?" his dermatologist friend asked, when, for a second time, he cornered her at the hospital. They were at the cafeteria, having coffee, and she looked at him with concern.

"I don't remember. Why?"

"Because moles that have hairs on them are almost always benign."

He closed his eyes. "I can't remember. It's just a blur."

"Why don't you call her then?"

"She'd think I was stupid."

"I think you'd live." She reached over and patted his hand. He noticed that she was wearing an indigo scarf that looked lovely against her blond hair. Also, she had a mole on the right side of her nose, a small brown mole he hadn't remembered seeing.

"Is that new?" he asked, touching it.

"No, I've always had it. Anyway, almost everyone in the world has a mole somewhere on their body. You, too, Dennis." And she touched a small brown spot on his wrist in a way that moved him. He asked her to dinner, but she shook her head. "You've just gotten divorced. Give it some time."

It was too cold to walk home, so he took the subway, and as he stood there, being jostled with the others, he began to see moles everywhere—erupting on faces, on hands that weren't wearing gloves. Their owners seemed calm, impervious, yet as he looked at the moles, he began to wonder if he had a moral obligation to speak to these people. His small amount of knowledge felt like a burden and that night he dreamt about Sharon's eyes staring past him towards a fixed and finite point—just like the eyes of certain terminally-ill patients who are able to see ahead to their very last moment in time. He woke in a sweat, and decided to call her, but the next day changed his mind, and wrote her a letter instead. He signed his full name—Dennis Gaviola—and used plain white paper, not his doctor's stationery:

Dear Sharon: I hope you won't think me untoward if I mention to you that the other night I happened to notice a mole on the inside of your thigh. It was a small blue mole, and I only bother to write, because I know that blue moles can sometimes be dangerous. Although I'm sure you probably already know about it, I couldn't walk around in good conscience without mentioning it to you. By the way, I really enjoyed meeting you and I hope we'll see each other again. Sincerely, Dennis Gaviola.

He wasn't sure about the phrase *I hope you won't think me untoward*. It had an oddly formal quality, and he decided to consult an old friend, an editor, who lived in Boston.

"I think it's ridiculous," the friend said, when he read the letter on the phone. "For God's sake, don't ever send it."

"But what if I took out that phrase?"

"It would still be ridiculous."

"Why?"

"Because. There's nothing wrong with her."

His friend sounded remote, safe in a happy marriage. "Terrible things can happen," he continued, "but they're never the things you worry about in advance."

═══════

He didn't mail the letter, but kept it by his bed, in its envelope, reading it over and over, trying to imagine that he was Sharon at the exact moment of opening it. He always saw her reading the letter fully clothed, except for once, when she was wearing his shirt, and her reaction was always the same—contempt. The letter became creased, began to look like a map, and twice he had to snatch it from his eight-year-old son. Finally he stuck it in his dresser drawer, and read it only occasionally. He never could decide about the phrase *I hope you won't think me untoward*.

═══════

Later that spring he met, and had an affair with, a woman who had no moles. Her name was Corazon Martinez, she was from Argentina, and an interpreter for the State Department. He had vowed he would never mention moles in her presence, but one day, to his own amazement, he said to her: "You have no moles!" and she answered, solemnly: "I know. I am completely unmarked." They were lying on her bed and Corazon sat up and looked at her skin as if trying to see it from a distance.

"Do you think moles are important?" he asked.

"Oh yes," she said. "Very. They're like keys to unknown cities. I've always wanted one."

═══════

That night he came home and tore up his letter to Sharon, bit by bit, piece by piece. It was like tearing up a love letter, written to him by someone else. When the letter was shredded, he burned it on the stove, and finally, mercifully, Sharon receded in his mind. He forgot about her, forgot about her mole, and was surprised when he saw her on the subway, about eight months later near Christmastime. It hadn't occurred to him that she would still exist, living an ordinary life, yet here she was opposite him, holding packages, wearing a dark blue coat—still with that smoldering sense of unavailable inner heat. She was staring into space and looked abstractedly, quietly happy.

The instant her saw her he remembered her mole. Indeed he had a graphic image of it, nestled on the inside of her thigh, a hidden eye, a secret pearl, surprising other lovers or—maybe she was married now—her husband. Sharon didn't notice him, didn't even look his way, and when she came to her stop, he waited for her to disappear. But as soon as the doors opened, he found himself racing to catch up with her. He reached her at the top of the stairs.

"Are you okay?" he said, when she turned to face him. "I've been meaning to call. I've been thinking about you."

"Oh, I'm okay," she said, smiling. "Even though I've been to hell and back."

"Was it your mole?" he blurted out, "was there anything wrong with it?" He looked at her eyes, and noticed, to his relief, that they didn't look like the eyes of a terminally-ill person at all. They were relaxed, somewhat dreamy, and seemed to stare ahead towards an indefinite, undefined point on the horizon. Now they turned to him, puzzled.

"My mole?" she said. "Is that all you can ask me about after all these months? Jesus. No. I mean I've finally gotten my divorce."

"I didn't know you were married."

"You didn't ask."

"But you didn't tell me!"

She smiled again, wryly, that heat still locked inside of her, and then she walked away, leaving him over twenty blocks from home. He began to walk—quickly, fiercely, with the sense of some new and unnamed burden, having nothing to do with her mole, or anything else he would ever be able to decipher.

THE LAST LADY WHO LOVED
HOWARD HUGHES

THE LAST LADY WHO LOVED HOWARD HUGHES SITS ON
her terrace on Malibu Beach, with her cat and a glass
of gin. She's old, nearly ninety, and is looking at the
beach where Howard once landed his plane. Yesterday
detectives came to visit her, but she's been questioned
so many times she's used to it, and is still talking to
them: "Howard couldn't stand me," she is saying, "but
it wasn't a personal thing, Howard couldn't stand
anybody. He hated the way people looked and he hated
the way people smelled and he hated the way people
tasted."

She turns to an invisible detective and asks:
"Wouldn't you like some gin?"

"No, I'm sorry," he answers, "I just never drink
on the job."

Her house is a modest beach house with a lot of windows. Yesterday, without any explanation, one of the detectives went inside and began rummaging through drawers of silverware and opening cookbooks filled with pressed flowers. She watched from the terrace, then asked the other detective to come inside. He came to the living room uneasily and sat on a bamboo chair.

"Some people say that Howard was enchanted," she said to him, "but he was only very strange. Much too strange to be enchanted." She opened an old cupboard and pulled out an enormous pair of brass scales.

"Do you know what this is?" she asked.

"No. What?"

"The scales for weighing women's derrières. Howard always made women sit on them before he made love because he was afraid he was going to be crushed. Finally I just said to him, 'Howard I promise I'll never be on top,' and then I went out and sold them."

"My God."

"Yes. I sold them at an auction. They're made of brass and come from Turkey. After I sold them, Howard got so angry, he bit my hand. Thank God Howard only weighed derrières, and not breasts. He said he trusted breasts to stay the same, but didn't have the same trust of derrières. Look you can see the scar."

The detective looked at the scar. It surrounded her lifeline like a picket-fence. "How terrible," he said. "It must have hurt."

The other detective was still rummaging through the kitchen. The lady addressed both of them and said: "Taking the scales was the only thing I ever did in the way of a crime. Anyway, everybody steals something. Haven't you?"

"Only when I was little," said the detective in the living room.

"What about your friend?"

"You'll have to ask him." He went over and looked at the scales. They were massive and deep. It was impossible to imagine how women had been weighed on them. "I just want to know one thing," he said. "If you sold them how come you got them back?"

"Because the auctioneer gave them to me when Howard died. Wasn't that kind? No one ever bought them, and he thought I might want a memento. Not that I wouldn't have wanted something else. But still, it was something."

The other detective was listening to the story from the kitchen. He looked skeptical and walked over to the scales. They were covered with Persian letters. The brass had a burnished gleam.

"You can't blame her for taking this," the other man said.

"No, of course you can't. It was a form of torture."

"Let's let it go, then," he said. "She doesn't have anything important here and the people who run that estate are kooks."

"I don't care," said the lady. "You can come and ask me questions anytime. The important thing about Howard is I loved him."

To his own surprise, the detective who had been rummaging in the kitchen bowed. "Madam," he said. "I have no doubt of that."

———

Today the detectives are silent and respectful. The last lady who loved Howard Hughes looks at the beach through her glass of gin and then she looks at the scales. She turns to one of the detectives and says: "Have you ever wondered why some of the heaviest things in the world seem light? Every day I notice, and it opens my eyes."

SILENCE

SHE LAY IN BED WITH KANSAS AROUND HER AND HEARD none of it. The birds were noiseless, the trees were noiseless, Erik was noiseless: She was sick and there was fluid in her ear.

Erik brought her orange juice and set it by the bed. She drank without hearing. Erik sat next to her. Which virus is it? he mouthed. Both, she said. Both? Yes. It's possible for someone to have both.

When the doctor had explained she would be deaf for a while, Erik brought her to his house: He was lonely in that town, and, when she had first come there, he'd seized her like a Viking taking a sad bride. With a grim face, he'd carried her suitcase over the green lawns until she found a place to stay, and now she lay on his bed reading Swedenborg's *Treatise on Angels.*

It was still in the house: The clocks beat rhythms she couldn't hear. The phone rang, like chimes beneath the sea. She answered it to hear the barely audible voice of Erik's mother, who thought she was the girls who fed the cat. Do you feed the cat? she asked.

＝＝＝＝

Swedenborg said angels always wore shoes: The highest angels wore gold shoes, the lowest angels wore red shoes, and the middle angels wore blue and silver shoes. Angels were careful about their shoes, even though they didn't lose things. And these weren't real shoes, Swedenborg explained, but essential attributes. She was reminded of her mother, who always seemed to be wearing shoes, even when she was naked.

She put down the book, startled, because Erik came in with orange juice. Your mother called, she said, without hearing her voice. Erik nodded.

Old plants, a legacy from his ex-wife, stood choking on the porch. Marbles that belonged to his sons rattled in Mason jars. His mother didn't know his wife lived in another town: It would break her heart to tell her, he explained.

＝＝＝＝

Erik got up from the bed and began to move toward the kitchen, stooped, inhabited by an old person. It was strange that her mother, who didn't live with a man, compared being without one to not wearing shoes. But as for herself, she went out with Erik for another reason: There was only one of everything in this town—one college, one drugstore, and one man. The other men were attached; and, if you failed to notice this, you lost your reputation. There was only one reputation, too, and its peregrinations were recorded in a ledger.

=======

While she lay in bed watching the hill made by her legs fade into dusk, Erik walked around the kitchen making Chinese food. Outside the town was calm: The one old lady floated in the gray light, and the one child played with the one dog. Erik had one wok and one menacing chopper from the People's Republic. He made noiseless Chinese chicken, crushing star anise and arranging ginger over snow peas. He put everything onto a tray and glided into the bedroom.

=======

At this hour, everyone ate one of something. The old lady ate a stewed apple, the child ate porridge. Only the students had coke and pizza and marijuana at the edge of town. There were twenty-seven hundred students and they had four of everything. Erik sat by her eating silently.

Later, he crawled into bed and they pounded together, like divers beneath the sea. She heard nothing—neither breath, nor flesh, nor heart. Erik whispered, forgetting she couldn't hear.

Sometimes, while Erik slept, she walked around the house. She found a piece of paper in his study that said: *Art is a collection of complexities: If only I cd. pierce one thing long enough to know its secret. . . .*

Erik was tall with a veil in front of his eyes. His vision occurred somewhere beyond his face, reminding her of Aaron—a junkie with a floating, veil-like stare. She had lived with Aaron in Greenwich Village, where he dealt dope, and, over the months, installed a floor in his slum apartment, board by board. Sometimes she found Aaron on the fire-escape with a brilliance pouring from his head as though he were about to die. He always wore a blue bathrobe and smiled like a child. She would pull him into the living room, and sit with him until morning.

═══   ═══

Now Erik came into the bedroom with a biography of Swedenborg. For you, he said. She tried to find where he was seeing her, somewhere in front of his eyes, and he sat by the bed waiting for her to talk. Finally she wrote, *Thanks for Swedenborg, sorry I can't hear you,* and he scribbled back, *Cilla when are you going to hear?* Then he turned the other way, because she was the only woman in town.

═══   ═══

According to Swedenborg, angels also got sick, but it was a deeper sickness—they lost their light. When angels lost their light, they withdrew to bright pools of air in the kingdom; and they put their fingers through their bodies, again and again. *Angels don't need pills,* she wrote jokingly. And she tried to locate Erik's vision, as though his eyes were two points on a triangle. *But what about more pills?* he wrote. *Why don't you call the doctor?*

═══   ═══

Her mother called: Erik's number had been relayed by a neighbor. While she tried to hear her mother, Erik came home with groceries and enormous, leather-bound books. Later, she opened one to an engraving of the largest ear she'd ever seen—almost a foot-and-a-half high, sprouting wild hairs. The inner chamber curved like a staircase and there were delicate things inside, labeled with letters of the alphabet. A secret feeling filled the room.

That night, Erik looked intently at the ear, lost in fascination, thinking she couldn't see—a voyeur with a portable peephole. He wasn't like Aaron who could sit on the fire-escape with his head pouring light. He was wavery and fragile, like a sheaf of wheat.

━━━━━

Papers from her students poured in, and she wrote comments with a soundless pen: "Luke—I think this piece suffers from lack of concrete imagery, but the ominous atmosphere is strong. For this reason, you don't need the phrase 'oh my God, the girl, the girl. . . .' This is implied. . . ." She stacked up the papers like pancakes and Erik rode them on his bicycle to her office.

━━━━━

Erik still brought orange juice and hung around her bed, but he was abstracted, obsessed with ears. More books appeared from the library and, next to his file on Browning, he kept a forest-green file of anatomical notes. One night she found the bed empty and walked to the study to see him asleep in a large pink blanket, convoluted and stiffened to form the shape of an ear. Erik was tucked in the shell-like cochlea, one long foot drooped over the lobe. Beyond his head were delicate instruments: Small hammers. Wooden anvils. Bones. They were smooth and it seemed quiet inside. She touched Erik's foot and went to bed, where she read that angels will forgetfulness to understand human affairs: Their memories are kept in the fire of their wings, and can, as God sees fit, be destroyed by a single flame.

THE NEW THIEVES

ONE NIGHT MY HUSBAND SAID: YOU MUST LEARN TO BE like one of the new thieves—they never steal, they add. They enter rooms without force and leave hairpins, envelopes, roses. Later they leave larger things like pianos; no one ever notices. You must learn to be like that woman in the bar who dropped her glove so softly I put it on. You must learn to be like that man who offered his wife so gently I thought we'd been married for seventeen years. You must learn to fill me with riches—so quietly I'll never notice. After saying this he draped himself in all my scarves and lay back in bed. What can I give you? I said, what do you really want? Nothing, I can tell you about, he said.

The next day I brought home a woman in camouflage, and placed her on top of our bed. She looked just like me and talked just like me and that night while I pretended to sleep, she made love to my husband. I thought I'd accomplished my mission, but as soon as she left, he said to me: I knew she wasn't you. I knew by the way she'd kissed.

I tried other things, but nothing eluded him— new shoes just like his old ones, scuffed in the same places, keepsakes from his mother, books he'd already read. He recognized everything and threw it away.

———

One rainy fall afternoon when I could think of nothing else to give him, I went into an elegant bar, the kind with leather chairs and soft lights. I ordered a glass of chilled white wine, and suddenly, without guile, there was instant understanding between me and the bartender. That night while my husband slept next to us, he and I made love, and the next morning he hung up his clothes in my husband's closet. Soon he moved in with us, walking like a cat, filling our rooms with objects. My husband never noticed, and now at night he lies next to us, thinking that he's the bartender. He breathes his air, dreams his dreams and in the morning when we all wake up, he tells me that he's happy.

USING THE CAR FOR BUSINESS

WHEN ALEXIS SAW A STRANGER GET INTO HER CAR, SHE didn't race to the phone and call the police. It all seemed so natural—like the time she'd been living in New York and a burglar came to her window and she thought he was going to wash it. It had taken a minute to realize who he was, and by the time she had, the man had run up the fire escape and she could hear his footsteps pounding on the roof. This time she had the same delayed reaction, only when she came to her senses, the car was gone. A bald-headed man in a maroon tie and a rumpled grey suit opened the unlocked door of her Cressida station wagon, revved up the engine, and drove it down the street. The maneuver was deft, dextrous, executed with grace. Where the car had been, the air now shimmered in darkness.

Alexis was a therapist. While the car was being stolen, she had been listening to a client tell a long and complicated dream about a wind-tunnel. For about thirty seconds after the car was gone, she stayed quite still, amazed and strangely fascinated. When the client paused, she righted herself and said:

"Excuse me, Jeremy, but my car's just been stolen. I just happened to look out the window and I saw this guy get into it and drive away. So I think I ought to do something. Like call the police."

"Sure," said Jeremy, looking irritated and vaguely startled. "Go ahead." He looked away from Alexis and at his feet, which were long and shapely: Jeremy was a dancer and always took off his shoes during sessions. "Go ahead and call," he said.

"My car's just been stolen," said Alexis, when the cop at her precinct answered the phone. "Some bald-headed man's just driven it down the street. It was all so natural. Maybe he made a mistake."

"Don't you wish he had," said the policeman. "Those guys with skeleton keys act so cool, like the car's just theirs and they're using it for business. Did you say you had your car keys?"

"Yes, they're in my pocket."

"Then there's no way the guy thought the car belonged to him."

━━━━━

Alexis hung up, and saw Jeremy looking at her searchingly. The look was unusual. Mostly Jeremy stared at his feet.

"Jeremy, are you having any feelings about being interrupted?" she asked.

"No. I was feeling sad about your car. It's a very strange feeling. Right in the middle of my stomach."

"Maybe it's about some loss of your own."

"No. It's about your car. It's strange, but I feel sad about it." He touched his stomach lightly, and Alexis noticed that a pervasive grey veil that always hovered around Jeremy's eyes was replaced by a steely gaze. He turned, looked out the window. Alexis looked too. Where her dark blue Cressida had been, there was now a yellow VW bug. Jeremy frowned and sighed. Suddenly he asked:

"Are you feeling sad about it, too?"

"No. Actually I'm not."

"How come? Didn't you like it? Wasn't there stuff in it you needed?"

"I don't know. I'll have to think."

Alexis thought. So many things were in the car's back seat: Her red silk scarf, the bag of roasted chestnuts, her daughter's favorite bear, a book on the emergence of the ego, plastic diapers, a bottle of wine. But all she felt was strange, light-hearted curiosity, as though the car belonged to someone else:

"No, Jeremy, I guess I'm not really feeling sad," she said. "I mean it's not that I don't want to find the car. But somehow I don't feel sad. Maybe I'm still surprised. Maybe I'll feel sad later."

"I know what you mean," said Jeremy. "I always feel that way with lovers. When it's over there's a kind of relief, and then later I miss them and I like that.What would you call that? Poignancy?"

"Poignancy's a very good word for it."

Jeremy nodded slowly, and the veil rose around his eyes again like mist. "The tunnel was very dark," he said, "and it was like I was just about to meet some-one." He paused abruptly and stared into space. "I was wearing this brown silk scarf and an olive-green trench coat I would die for. I *liked* the way I was dressed."

After Jeremy left, Alexis called her insurance company and told them about her car. Then she called her hus-band Caleb who taught music history at the univer-sity. He was listening to a recording of Grieg's *Nocturne,* and the music made her sad. "Caleb," she said—shaping her voice to match the sadness— "something terrible's happened. My car's been stolen."

"My God," said Caleb. "How?"

"I don't know. Some bald-headed guy just got in-to it and drove it away. I saw it from my window. I was with a client."

Caleb turned off Grieg. "My God, I had a musical score in there! A flute concerto that someone sent me from England! For God's sake! It's in the car!"

"You mean you just *left* it in my car?"

"Sure. I thought it was safe. My God, Alexis, didn't

you run to the phone? Didn't you call the police?"

"The truth is, it took me a minute or so. I only get a dollar-and-forty cents a minute for being a tabula rasa—it's not like I can just snap out of it. Anyway, my client was telling me a dream. I waited until he stopped."

"What do you mean you waited? Weren't you upset?"

"Yes. I was upset. And I waited."

Caleb poured himself more coffee—Alexis could hear gurgling over the phone. "Aren't you supposed to set an example for your clients?" he asked. "Aren't you supposed to teach them about passion? What is this jerk going to think if he's telling you a dream and you just watch someone steal your car?"

"I'm not supposed to teach people anything," said Alexis, feeling a protective rush. "I allow them to be *themselves*."

"Well I'm myself and I'm pissed," said Caleb. He drank more coffee and then hung up. Alexis stayed at her desk, holding the phone to her ear. Since she'd made the call herself, there was no dial-tone, just an uneasy silence, broken by scratches and squeaks.

Alexis felt terrible about the musical score. She knew exactly what it looked like, because Caleb brought so much old music home—yellow, delicate paper, frail spidery notes. She could see it in the back seat of her car, mingling with the books and diapers. She could see the bald-headed man regarding it curiously, throwing it away. She knew that for a while Caleb would bring home no more precious things—no ancient musical scores, no rotting viola da gambas, no torn opera programs from London pawnshops. The house would be less cluttered: Caleb might even agree there were too many things in the world and having one of them disappear, even if it happened to be a car, could only be cause for relief. As Alexis thought this, she began to confuse Caleb with Jeremy, as though Caleb were sitting in her office in his stocking feet, a veil lifted from his eyes. In fact he never visited her office, hated going without shoes, and his veil—for of course he had one—was around his ears. It was a strange place for a musicologist to have a veil; whenever she tried to talk to him about it, he insisted he had perfect pitch.

While Alexis was thinking these things a stern voice rose from the phone and told her to hang up. As soon as she did a policeman called with news that they'd found her car. "It was by a warehouse near the bay, with the door unlocked and the key under the driver's seat. There must have been a foul-up with the rendezvous."

Alexis caught her breath. For a moment the car seemed too close, too fragile, precariously near the water. "Was there an old piece of music in it? Something on very old paper?"

"Yes, as a matter of fact there was. It looks like some antique."

In the following months, Alexis was called to inspect several police line-ups. She liked being ushered to a darkened room where bald-headed men were assembled on an empty stage. The men lined up impassively, looking detached, daring her to discover them. She never did and was always glad.

"What's the scoop?" Caleb always asked when she came home. "Did you find him? did you turn him in?" He was writing an article linking the musical score to chamber music, and looked safe and intelligent, close to the 18th century. He'd forgiven Alexis about Jeremy's dream, and Alexis smiled vaguely when asked about the bald-headed men. "I'm sure the real one went to Mexico. I mean . . . wouldn't *you* if you stole a car?"

After one visit to the police station, Alexis went to a burrito parlor, sat at a table in the back, nursed a glass of cheap red wine and watched punk kids, bag ladies, close-knit Mexican families. At one point the door opened and a bald-headed man walked in, tentatively, then briskly, heading straight for the bar. He wore a rumpled tie, rumpled suit, and had the seedy elegance of grand deteriorating buildings. Alexis looked at him, he looked back, and for a moment she felt a curious collapse of space, as though she could reach out in an instant and touch him from where she was. Not that she ever would, the way he was staring. She drank the last of her wine and drove home without any headlights. "You could have killed yourself," said Caleb, when she came into the house.

WORK AND TIME

MARY WAS RUMMAGING THROUGH HER DESK, LOOKING for aspirin. Her head was splitting, and all she could find were paperclips. "Harry?" she called into the next cubicle. "Harry? Do you have any aspirin?" "No," said Harry, "but I've cooked up something I think you'll like." He walked into her office and threw a piece of yellow legal paper on her desk. "Look at this!" he said, sounding pleased. Mary looked. It was a work-time problem in Harry's handwriting. She read:

If it takes 1 man working 1 hr a day 2½ days to write a 3-line poem for a Hallmark greeting card, how long will it take 3 men working 7 hrs a day to write a 7-line poem? 8 men working 9 hrs a day? 2 men working ½ a week? if there are a total of 11 men and 1 man works 8 hrs and the rest work 3 hrs how long will it take to write a 4-line poem?

    "Do you like it?" said Harry. He leaned toward Mary in his floppy, loose-jointed way.
    "I'm not sure I do," Mary said. "I mean don't

you think it's sort of pandering to my unhappiness?"

"Pandering to your unhappiness! Well blimey be!" said Harry, in a Cockney accent. He left the room, laughing.

Mary looked at the piece of paper and sighed. She and Harry worked for a textbook company that specialized in math books for junior high school kids. Harry thought up the problems. Mary edited them. Harry was married to Greta who wore panty hose to bed and wanted to go home to Holland. Mary was married to Ian, who had been working on a novel ever since they'd gotten married.

"My God," Mary once said to Harry at lunch. "Do you know how long I've been at this lousy job? Eight hours, five days a week, for seven years. Minus weekends and a few vacations. And for what? Two-hundred-and-fifty thousand dollars while he sits at home."

They were having dim-sum in a shadowy Chinese restaurant. A mushroom fell from Harry's chopsticks onto the floor.

"Why did you agree to support him?" he asked, pushing the mushroom under the table with his foot.

"Because the Gothic he wrote before we were married took him less than a year. But now he'd doing something *serious*." Mary stared at Harry's shirt. The mushroom had left a stain near one of the buttons. She longed to touch it.

When Mary came home Ian was at his desk, staring out the window at some bougainvilleas. She stormed into his study, threw one of Harry's math problems in front of him.

"Read this," she commanded. "Out loud!"

Ian shrugged. He read: "If it takes one man, working eight hours a day five days a week, 267 days to write a 1,078 page historical novel, how long will it take three men, working seven days a week, to write a novel of half that length?" He cleared his throat. "If four more men were added to the project, but they worked only four hours a day three days a week, would it take more or less time? What about seven men working one day a week?"

"What do you think?" said Mary.

"I think it's shameful," said Ian. "What are kids supposed to think—that art happens on an assembly line? Whoever thought this up?"

"Harry. Harry Lipmann."

"Well Harry's a fool. A royal and unconscionable fool."

"I knew you would say that!" said Mary, wriggling out of her panty hose and going to the kitchen. "You like to think art is mystical."

"I don't! It happens in a different kind of time!"

Mary didn't answer. She put on a blue-and-red striped apron and began to peel carrots. It was her turn to cook, even though she didn't see why she should, with Ian staring at the bouganvilleas all day. While she was peeling Ian came in and nuzzled her shoulder. "Are you getting it on with Harry Lippmann?" he asked.

"No. I'm not getting it on with *anyone.*" Mary swooped from under Ian's arm. She threw the carrots in an oversized pot.

———

At dinner both of them were silent. Mary was calculating how long it was taking them to eat, and Ian was brooding. Finally he said: "Who was he?"

"Who?" said Mary. She was eating a radish and her whole being was absorbed in eating it.

"The author in the time-study problem," said Ian, "the guy who was able to write a novel in less than a year. Who was he?"

"I don't know. Harry made him up."

"You mean no real person ever wrote a novel that long in that short a time?"

"I didn't say that. I just said that probably Harry made this particular person up." Mary picked up another radish. It took less than a second to disappear.

"Well Harry is performing a terrible disservice

to children. What are they going to think? That art is like cartoons they see on television?"

"I have no idea what they're going to think. We're just trying to teach them math." Mary gave Ian a veiled look. She stood up. "Tonight it's your turn to do the dishes."

━━━━━

While Ian did the dishes, Mary weeded the garden. They were on the top floor of a duplex, so when Ian looked down, Mary seemed small, almost rodent-like, bending over the vegetable plot with frantic intensity. Their garden was overgrown, ivy crawling every-where. Ian finished the dishes and sat beside Mary on the grass.

"Do you know what I'm thinking?" he asked while she pulled at weeds.

"No." She sounded uninterested.

"I'm thinking about how long it would take to pull up all those tulips. And then how long it would take to put them back."

"For God's sakes, don't pull up the tulips. They're *annuals*."

"Actually I was thinking about planting roses. Those huge yellow kind."

"Roses are labor-intensive. They're very hard to take care of." Mary gathered the weeds into a bundle, tossed them into the compost, and went upstairs. In a moment she was in her bathrobe, sitting on their bed, editing Harry's problems for a seventh grade workbook. God, Harry's math is bad, she thought. In some ways he's really a creep. She was just about to turn seventy-seven seconds into a year when Ian came in with an enormous bundle of tulips. He dumped them on the bed and she was surrounded by red flowers, dark earth.

"What did you do this for?" she asked.

"I don't know. I wanted to bring you flowers."

"You wanted to bring me flowers? Do you know how long these took to plant?"

"Come on Mary, I left in the bulbs. Give me a break."

"But why? why did you do this?" Mary looked at Ian as though he were a dangerous weed.

"I wanted to give you a present."

"You did? Well why don't you give me a *real* present? Like a necklace." Mary got up, gathered the tulips in her arms. She felt oddly festive, like a beauty queen.

"You really want a necklace?"

"Yes. A lapis necklace in a silver setting. Didn't you ever know that?"

"Of course I didn't."

"Of course is right! It's the material world that's beyond you." Mary swept out of the room, yelling over her shoulder, "You think everything's made out of words. Don't you?"

"You don't know what I think," yelled Ian. "You don't know what I think at all!" He looked at the black earth on the white spread, decided not to brush it off, followed Mary to the kitchen where she was arranging tulips in vases and jars. "All our flowers," she muttered with a pinched intense look. "All the flowers in our garden. . . ."

They glared over the flowers. Ian left. He didn't say where he was going, but Mary knew he was going to visit Cindy Hermann, who lived on the same block and had been writing a thesis on the mating habits of salmon for the past eight years. Two misfits, she thought, dialing Harry's number.

———

Ian was turned on to Cindy even though she looked a little like a salmon. She lived in a garret with green curtains and sometimes watched soap operas during the day. He never visited without a reason. Tonight he brought back the camera he'd borrowed as an excuse to see her last time.

"What's up?" Cindy asked when he knocked on the door.

"Nothing," said Ian, "just returning this." He gave her the camera and pulled a chair through a rubble of papers. For a moment he felt superior because all his work was in files.

"How are the salmon?" he asked, drawing his chair close to Cindy.

"Getting there. Getting upstream." It was what Cindy always said. It was what she had said five years ago when he first came over with some old computer discs he had wanted to give away. She had just washed her hair and smelled sweet and steamy. She wrapped a dark maroon towel around it and offered Ian some port. "How's Mary doing?" she asked.

"Angry. Like always. She thinks I'm taking too much time." Ian took a sip of port. It made him feel solid and tranquil. He didn't have to explain what Mary was angry about: They'd had this conversation before.

"That's nice," said Cindy, pouring herself a glass. "No, really, I mean it. I wish I had someone to nag me. Nagging is a form of love. You miss it when it's not happening." She released the towel and her red hair fell around her shoulder—dark, like seaweed, because it was wet.

"What about Arnie? Doesn't he nag you?" Arnie was Cindy's boyfriend.

"Arnie nags about other things. Like my sense of order."

"Your sense of order? I thought you were organized."

Cindy shrugged and Ian didn't ask. He wished he could have an affair with Cindy, the kind where you crawl into bed on rainy, unproductive afternoons; but he never would because Cindy and Mary had been friends at college, and besides, it was enough to see her unhappy fish-blue eyes as she frowned at a graph she picked up from the floor. Ian leaned over her shoulder. The graph charted an underwater spawning route.

"Do they really swim upstream?"

"Yes. Why wouldn't they?"

"I don't know. Just wondered." Ian poured himself more port. "What do you think? Will the good life ever be popular?"

"Not with me," said Cindy, with such ferocity he was sorry he had asked. In a moment, he got up, kissing her on the cheek, and saying:

"Come to dinner sometimes. And bring Arnie, too, if he's still in the picture."

———

When he came home, the living room was exploding with tulips. There were mason jars around the hearth, jam jars on the mantle, vases on the bookcase.

"Hello, Ian," Mary called from the bedroom, using his name formally, as though she didn't know him. And then she cried out, in the same formal voice: "Guess what? I've decided to quit my job. I'm not going to edit this math crap anymore."

"You're what?" said Ian, walking to the bedroom slowly.

"I'm not going to edit this math crap anymore." Mary was standing in the middle of the room. Her papers were scattered on the floor.

"I'm quitting!" she cried, raising her hands like a prophet. "I'm quitting my job. I've had it! Up to here!"

"I gather." Ian stood cautiously be the door. "But what's going to happen? What are you going to do?"

"I don't know. Harry's going to lend me some money for a while, and then . . . I'll see." Mary let her arms drop. Ian stepped into the room.

"Come on, tell me. Are you getting it on with him?" He walked on a piece of paper, maybe something Harry had written.

"No. He just feels sorry for me, that's all. I mean I've worked at this job for over seven years, and it's going to take about ten minutes to quit it. Isn't that depressing? Just like eating a meal that's taken hours to cook." Mary took their gilt-framed mirror from the wall and set it on the floor. "I'm bringing this to Harry," she said. "I want to give him something and his kids broke their mirror last week. I think he and Greta will like it." She sat on the bed and sighed.

"Do you really think you ought to? Quit your job, I mean? Certain things just don't happen overnight. They take time." Ian came over to the bed, reached inside Mary's bathrobe, began to massage her back, whispering, "Mary, who's fed-up with Ian, must travel light-years away to quit her job. If it takes a flea three hundred years to reach her office, how long will it take

Mary in her blue Volkswagen bug?" His voice floated insider her head, weightless, blurred, lost in lunar light. He kissed her, nuzzling against her cheek.

"Don't," said Mary, "please don't." She ducked from under his arm, made a show of trying to get up, but already was remembering the tulips—all red against the creamy white spread. "What am I going to do?" she said to Ian. "What in God's name am I going to do?" "Relax," he said, "and I'll tell you. . . ." Mary leaned against his shoulder and relaxed: His advice took the form of a story and was filled with extraordinary people, people who lived in amusement parks and took years, sometimes eons, to begin their lives.

THE SEXUAL GEOGRAPHY OF CAPITAL CITIES

HE WAS SEVENTY-TWO, A MASTER SPY, AND SHE WAS twenty-four, fresh from training with the CIA. They met in eastern Europe on a mission, and when the mission was over she begged him to train her in counter-espionage. It was a surprise when he said he would. Rumor had it that he wasn't taking pupils.

The training was rigorous. She had to meet him everyday at a viaduct near a marble quarry, seven miles from the city. She had to greet him in a foreign accent, then walk through the immense quarry, identifying stones. At times she had to act as though she were alone, at other times as though she were with a large group of people. He stood at a distance, hunched over in his trench coat, taking notes.

He was a mole many times over—working for and against himself so often it no longer mattered to anyone what he was doing. She saw him make several phone calls to the same person at once, speaking in different languages. She saw him walk through traffic twisted like a Möbius strip. Once she told him she knew he was a mole, and he shrugged and said he wasn't.

One evening he said she'd passed various tests and was ready to learn the secret of counter-espionage—discovering the sexual geography of capital cities. She asked if this had to do with phallic monuments and womb-like rotundas, but he shook his head. "No, not at all. Those are crude sexual symbols that fuel politicians in their war games. Sexual geography involves luminous boundaries, something that makes a place perfect for assignations."

"Like a park?"

"Sometimes, but not always."

"A viaduct!"

"Often. But certain viaducts don't work."

"Places near water!"

"Close, but not inclusive."

They were in a cafe and he was stirring his espresso. When he swirled the spoon to the right more coffee appeared; when he swirled it to the left it vanished. He saw her look at the cup and said: "You've noticed. Such knowledge leads to powers."

In the following weeks he walked her around the city blindfolded, asking her to find places imbued with sexual geography. They went to fountains, viaducts, parks, eavesdropped on conversations. She got to know the sound of running water, could tell how many spouts a fountain had. But she couldn't identify sexual geography.

One day they stopped in a park surrounded by

a wrought-iron fence, filled with leaves. The park, opposite the government treasury building, was named after seven martyrs who had been shot on the steps during the war. He led her to the gate and made her touch the stone that bore their names. She felt each letter, couldn't translate a thing. "It's in Latin!" he said. "You're failing miserably."

He removed the blindfold and his enormous eyes bored into her. "Do you know right now the most amazing secret is being exchanged on that park bench? By those two men with briefcases! They look like they're arguing but they're exchanging maps! And someone else is watching them from a pear tree! This place is rife with sexual geography."

She looked at the officials in grey suits, a stone equestrian statue, the pear tree, benches, scattered newspapers. "It all seems so ordinary," she said.

"It is ordinary," he answered. "As ordinary as a beer bottle." He thrust a piece of paper in her hands, blindfolded her again. "Write down everything you hear. I'll be back." He disappeared. She waited. Footsteps. Sounds of paper crumpling. Then, from behind her, an argument between two women about the best butcher in the city: "Zzerzo!" said one. "Chzlis," said the other.

She wrote down everything, uncertain how to spell the butcher's names. The women stopped talking. Silence. From another part of the park, a male voice said: "You must observe him very carefully. You know it can take six months to find the perfect time to kill someone: Watch how he walks. Whether he takes one lump of sugar or two. Everything depends on details."

"You're right, of course," said a woman's voice. "But with him there will never be a perfect moment. He's never alone. Always bustling, hurrying. To this shop and that. Buying. Bargaining. It's impossible."

More paper crumpling. Then the first voice: "Keep a picture of him in your mind. That's what I did with the Armenian—he was difficult, always acting like a tourist. I got him when he was doing his laundry."

She took off her blindfold. At the far end of the park she could see a man in dark glasses and a woman in a raincoat bending over a book of stamps: Too far away to be audible. Yet she knew she'd heard them talking. She walked over to them, asked what time it was. The man stared at her sharply.

"Were you listening to us?" he asked.

"No."

"How can we be sure?"

"By this," she said, lifting a hand to her mouth and blowing them both a kiss. They smiled, blew kisses back, returned to their book of stamps. From the other side of the park the argument about butchers continued: "Tvinich is the worst! His meat is like leather." "But Losolo is dirtier. And a cheat."

She walked back to her bench, trembling. The park was luminous: Benches glimmered, boundaries blurred. But the master was nowhere to be seen. She looked for him on the street, in trees, near the fountain. Finally she spotted him on the steps of the treasury building, eating an apple. She began to walk towards him, but suddenly he appeared from behind, tapping her on the shoulder.

"Where was I?" he asked.

"Everywhere!" she answered.

THE SECOND HUSBAND

MY SECOND HUSBAND, AARON, IS WEDGED SOMEWHERE
between my first husband, Dan, and my third husband,
Walker. Those two men are clear and distinct, and
whenever I think of them, I can always imagine what
they are doing—Dan asleep, his hairy shoulders rising
above the blankets like epaulets, Walker, ever wakeful,
looks at maps. These two men are obedient to the com-
mands of time, as is my fourth husband, Malcolm, who
is in our living room, reading. But as for Aaron, I can
never imagine what he is doing, or even where he is:
He remains my past like a segue, a half-note, and if I
imagine him at all he is walking in thin air, looking at
nothing in particular.

Aaron had a singular appeal: He always seemed awe-
struck. He was blond, delicate, and once spent a long
hot summer putting a floor in his slum apartment,
board by board. I watched him put in that floor, yet

often confuse him with other men who were also good carpenters. His face is fused with other faces, faces that are more distinct—and indeed, for a long time after we were divorced, I forgot that we were ever married. The memory came back after Malcolm and I had come back from a two-day honeymoon in the high Sierras. I was thinking about my most recent wedding when suddenly I remembered being in Manhattan City Hall, next to an unknown man. . . . And then I remembered a narrow walk-up apartment in Greenwich Village, near the Hudson River, and then Aaron's flat, with its wonderful hard-wood floor, part of which was a false floor concealing bundles of marijuana. It was then that I remembered Aaron, and realized I had been married to a drug dealer for all of three months. My God, I thought, sitting up in bed.

I looked around our book-strewn bedroom. My previously-third (but now, I realized, fourth) husband was lying next to me. Moonlight fell across our bed and illuminated his face, which looked peaceful. For a minute I couldn't remember his name. When I did, I shook him gently. "Have you ever been married before?"

"Don't wake me," he said from the depths of sleep.

———

I forgot about Aaron, consigned him to the past. He lived in those archives for a month, and then a friend told me that one night she also woke up with the memory of having been previously married. Details came back slowly and the features of the other husband were indistinct. Still, she was able to remember that he had a childlike charm, talked his way into deals, then got out of them.

"Was his name Aaron?" I asked.

"No," she said. "His name was Henry."

After we talked I wrote Aaron a letter (which I'll never mail) thanking him for everything he gave me, which was, among other things, a sense of mystery about my past. But this wasn't the end of the matter: A few days later I was walking down the street, and a man looked at me strangely. It wasn't a leer, it was a look of recognition and I nodded and hurried past him. The moment I got home, I called my friend. "Listen," I said, "are you sure Henry is the only one you forgot about marrying?"

"Oh no," she said. "I'm not sure at all."

"Doesn't it bother you?"

"Yes, as a matter of fact it does. In fact, whenever I meet someone for what I think is the first time, I panic. Like: have I seen his dirty socks? Does he know what I look like naked? That sort of thing."

"And how about children?" I asked. "Do you think you've ever had any others besides the ones you have?"

There was a pause. "No. I don't think so.

Somehow I think you'd remember children. Don't you?"

I wasn't so sure. There is a kind of generic child that can easily be forgotten or confused with other children, a child like mine with a round face, and a smooth unworried expression over a glass of milk. "No, I don't think you necessarily would. In some ways kids are pretty much the same."

While we talked I could hear her moving about her kitchen. She was making lentil soup for dinner, celebrating a settled life. Suddenly she said to me: "Listen, don't ever tell anyone this, but once I think I slept with a man I'd forgotten."

"What do you mean?"

"I mean I ran into him in the supermarket and we ended up in a motel. We didn't spend much time together. It was as though we didn't need any introductions." She laughed and sounded nervous.

"How could you know?" I said. "I mean if you've forgotten him, then how could you remember?"

"I don't know. There was this strange sort of pull. Like gravity."

"And did he remember you?"

"God. I don't know." She sounded tired. "Hey, please don't tell."

As soon as I hung up my husband came into the kitchen and began to poke around the refrigerator, bringing out carrots, onions, peppers. "What were you talking about?" he asked.

"Oh, nothing. Just the ways of the world."

"Really? I don't think so." His eyes had a piercing quality. "I think you were talking about your other husbands."

"Oh no. I really don't think about Walker or Dan."

"I don't mean that," he said, waving me away with his hand, which held a Chinese cleaver. "I mean the other ones. Those guys you don't remember. Don't worry, it's not a big deal, I've had other wives and I think of them in my sleep. But I never remember their names." He smiled at me generously. "I figure I've been married about fifteen times."

In a sense I wasn't surprised. Angry. Jealous. But not surprised. "What were they like, your wives?" I asked.

"Honestly, I don't remember. The most vivid one was an advice nurse named Dodie who worked at St. Vincent's when I was an intern, and knew everything. Like what time it was in Tokyo. Or whether Chaucer had ever had children. Finally she left nursing and went into film-making. Anyway, don't worry. You're the best." He came over and put his arms around me.

I wanted to tell him that he was the best. But Aaron was in my heart, his face enclosed in light. "Were you *really* married all those times?" I asked.

"Oh, that's just an estimate. Like I said, I don't remember their names or where we lived or anything about them. It's only a guess." He found some yogurt, took a couple of bites, and began to chop vegetables for dinner. He looked strong, inscrutable, and a little sad, as if all his marriages had worn him out. "How many times were you married that *you* forgot?" he asked. "Come on, tell the truth."

"Only once. You're really the fourth."

"And who's the one you forgot? Do you remember?"

"Oh, sort of. . . . A semi-criminal drug-dealer. Very charming. It's kind of a blur."

"What did he look like?"

"I don't remember. Blond, I guess."

"Cute?"

"Sort of."

"*Very* cute." This was a statement.

"No, really, he's all in a blur. Like I said: a semi-criminal type. Before I had limits."

I was spared having to say anything more because our son came in the kitchen with a toy I'd never seen—a green plastic monster with a red mask and a spear: I was appalled.

"Where did you get that?" I asked him.

"You gave it to me."

"No, I didn't! I'd never let something like that in our house. What is it?"

"A Ninja turtle."

"What's that?"

"Well, it's this dude," he said. And then he told us how the turtle had been living in a sewer with his friends when some bad guy poured slime all over them and they mutated into five-feet-tall adolescents with Ninja fighting skills. He was still holding the turtle who carried several spears.

"Why did you buy him this thing?" I said, turning to my husband. "It's a violent toy. I don't want it in the house."

"I didn't buy it," he said, "I thought *you* did."

We looked at each other, thinking the same thing.

"Who bought that for you?" I asked our child.

He looked puzzled, genuinely puzzled, and his eyes traveled deep into mine as if trying to retrieve something. I realized then that he easily had a hundred mothers, all of whom he loved, none of whom he remembered. I leaned over and gathered him up in my arms.

HYPERVENTILATION

ALMOST AS SOON AS THE PASTA WAS BROUGHT TO THE table one of the guests began to hyperventilate and asked to be excused. He was a tall high-strung man in his middle thirties and it wasn't he first time he had hyperventilated at the house of this particular couple. The hostess sent him an ill-willed glare. The host, however, was sympathetic.

"Poor Jonathon," he said after he disappeared, "he's so exhausted and the kids are driving him crazy." He was referring to the students in the art school where Jonathon and he both taught. "Just the other day this woman came up to him in the hall and asked if he would please mind strangling her. He thought she was crazy and then all these people began to clap and he realized it was a performance piece. The terrible thing was he didn't *get* it. You know Jonathon, he has this terrific sense of irony, but he didn't get it."

"Do you really think that happened?" said one of the guests. "Do you really think those kids would be so cruel?" The guest was trying not to look at the fusilli, steaming in a blue-and-white bowl. The hostess had cooked it *al dente* and soon it would have the consistency of cold rubber.

"Of course," said the host. "To those kids everything's an event. Except me: I'm the dean." He laughed and gestured toward the fusilli. "Should we serve it?" he asked, raising an eyebrow.

"No," said the hostess in the silent language of couples. "This time I want Jonathan to eat my food."

Jonathon's girlfriend, Ashley, a spindly-legged woman who looked like Orphan Annie, saw the signal in an instant. "Excuse me," she said, "I must see to Jonathon." She bolted from her seat and raced down the zig-zag hall filled with photographs of construction sites. Jonathon was sitting on the toilet with his pants on and his eyes closed, breathing deeply, furtively, as though the air were meant for someone else. Ashley knelt by the toilet and put her hands on Jonathon's knees.

"What in God's name are you doing?" she asked. "Are you stoned? Did you take something before we left?" Jonathon opened his eyes. They were wide, like someone else was holding them open.

"No. I just forget to breathe, that's all. Or I breathe too much. I'm not sure which." Jonathon looked around the bathroom, inhaling the sea-green tiles, the towels staggered artfully on a rack. "Why can't we live this way?" he asked. "They do it in such good taste."

"Because we have different values, that's why.

We buy books. We like to travel. Anyway, do you really like it?" Ashley picked up a brass spyglass on the edge of the sink and looked through it to see a sea-green wastebasket, a sea-green rubber duck, and a plastic shower curtain with a map of the world on it.

"Yes. I mean I think I like it. But probably I don't." Jonathon was breathing normally now. Ashley touched his arm.

"Are you ready to come out?"

"No, it's not like I'm breathing automatically or anything. It's like I have to think about it." He looked at Ashley sternly. "I'm not like other people. I don't have automatic functions. I have to *think*."

"Well let's go out anyway. It must seem really odd to them, our going to the bathroom at every party. They probably think we pee together. Or make love. Or snort coke." Ashley spoke abtractedly, spun around the bathroom, looking for solutions. "What's this?" she asked, bumping against the handle of a utility closet that was built into the wall. Her body jostled the handle loose, and several 17th-century wigs tumbled out. They were followed by a stiff purple brocade evening dress that looked occupied from the waist down, a walking stick, a mask, a corset, a silver reticule. "My God! What *is* all this?"

"From the play," said Jonathon dully. "That Molière thing the school did last year. You know them. They keep everything: Pack rats." He knelt on the floor and put on one of the wigs—a tower of silver curls with an artificial nightingale on top. "How do I look?" he asked, holding the gown to his chest with one hand and reaching for the door with the other. An evil triumphant look entered his eyes. "Shall we go out?"

"Jonathon, for God's sake take that off." Ashley shook him by the shoulders. "You will *not* go out in that. We will *not* have a repeat performance."

"Of what?"

"Never mind. Just take it *off*."

"Okay," said Jonathon, "I just wanted to add some levity." He took off the wig and his breathing became labored again. He resumed his seat on the toilet.

"How come you can't breathe here?" Ashley demanded, kneeling on the floor and cramming the wigs into the closet. And the dress, which popped out like a disobedient ghost. "How come you always breathe at other people's parties?" she asked, slamming the dress back inside, stuffing in the silver reticule, the mask, the corset, the walking stick. She leaned hard against the closet door until it clicked shut.

"I *don't* breathe at other people's parties."

"Sure you do. You breathe at Bob and Joanna's parties. And at the Motlers'. You breathe at them just fine."

"Okay, you're right. I do breathe there. It's all this hi-tech crap around this damned loft. Fiberglass aggravates my asthma."

Ashley looked unimpressed. "You don't have asthma. You went to the doctor, and he said you don't."

"I'm sorry to tell you this Ashley," said Jonathon solemnly, "but there's a rare kind that's hard to diagnose. I read about it in the *Merck Manual.* It's called *apernative asthma.* That's why I can't have sex."

"But we just did! It was great."

"No. I mean in the morning. I can't breathe."

"Jonathon, for God's sake. You won't even talk to me in the morning. It doesn't have anything to do with asthma." Ashley walked away from the closet cautiously. The door did not open. She picked up a conch shell and held it to the light. "We're living out of boxes," she remarked, somewhat absently, "and they have all this crap in their bathroom."

"The other reason my asthma is worse,"— Jonathon continued as if Ashley hadn't spoken—"is because of what happened with that student in the hall. I was freaked: and there's more to it than people know."

"What do you mean?"

"I mean I got my revenge, that's what I mean."

Ashley looked quickly at her watch—a black watch with a globe where four o'clock should be. "What do you mean revenge?" she said. The word sounded dark. She picked up a piece of jade that was lying on the sink. Smooth and green. It could have been soap.

"Don't you want the details? They're pretty ugly."

"No, I really don't. I just want to get through this evening." Ashley looked in the mirror and saw that her eyes looked frightened. There was a cake of Cynthia's eye-shadow on the sink—silver-gold, the shadow of Egyptian queens. She smudged some on her lids. "Listen, I'm going out, will you be okay?" Without waiting for an answer she opened the door and stepped into the hall. It was dark, except for one down-light, and she paused. In the dining room one of the guests was saying—"What I don't understand is why he comes to these things at all. I mean if he's not the social type, then why does he bother?" Ashley turned and knocked loudly on the door, commanding silence from the people at the table. "Are you coming out now?" she asked. Her voice sounded flat and far away. "Jonathon!" she cried. "Are you coming out?"

There were footsteps in the hall. It was Mark, the host. "Is there a problem?" he asked putting a hand on Ashley's arm, pressing softly. He stared at her with concern and she was forced to look at his eyes and remember the student in the hall. Mark was eight years older than Ashley and handled his lust by being avuncular. His regard was pensive, kind. Ashley made another show of knocking on the door. "Jonathon!" she cried. "Jonathon!" She opened the door a crack and squeezed inside. Jonathon was sitting on the edge of the bathtub looking serene. He, too, had put on some of Cynthia's eye make-up, and was reading an art-flyer.

"Well, it's passed," he said. "I can breathe now without having to think about it."

"Good," said Ashley. "Because they're wondering."

She noticed the silver-gold shadow upon his lids. "For God's sake. Will you take that off?"

"Wait. I'm getting my bearings." Jonathon stood up slowly, eased his feet to the floor, patted the shower curtain with the map of the world. "How would you like to see Guatemala every time you took a shit?" he asked. Ashley didn't laugh. She took some Kleenex, made Jonathon hold still while she wiped off the shadow. "Listen," she said. "I want to know something. What did you do to that student? Did you hurt her?"

"Nothing. I thought about coming after her with a rope and pretending I was going to strangle her. But I decided not to. In the interests of art."

"You mean you made it up?"

"Yes. You wanted a reason."

"Then go to hell."

"Oh for godssake, Ashley. The truth is, I don't have a reason. I don't even know if I have apernative asthma. This is just one of those places where I can't seem to breathe, that's all." Jonathon paused, looked around the bathroom. "You know what I discovered?" he said. "I discovered they have a false floor. Look! Those tiles are uneven. I bet they keep coke down there."

"I don't give a damn," said Ashley, who never wanted to spend another minute in the bathroom. She picked up the sea-green rubber duck and made it squeak. "How fucked," she said. "They have a duck, but they don't have kids." "Yes," Jonathon agreed, "it's crazy." They smiled in sudden agreement. Ashley opened the door, Jonathon offered her his arm and together they walked to the center of the loft. The fusilli was being served. Jonathon slid into his seat.

"To breath," he said, raising his glass.

POLAND

HER HUSBAND DIED SUDDENLY OF A HEART-ATTACK right in the middle of writing a poem. He was only thirty-eight, at the height of his powers—and people felt he had a great deal more to give, not just through his poetry but through the way he lived his life. His second wife, who was nearly ten years younger, found the poem half-finished, moments after he died, and put it in her pocket for safekeeping. She'd never liked his poetry, nor did she like the poem, but she read it again and again, as if it would explain something. The poem was about Poland. It was about how her husband kept seeing Poland in the rear-view mirror of his car, and how the country kept following him wherever he went. It was about fugitives hiding in barns, people eating ice for bread. Her husband had never been to Poland. His parents had come from Germany, just before World War II, and she had no sense that Poland meant anything to him. This made the poem more elusive, and its elusiveness made her sure that it contained something important.

Whenever she read the poem, she breathed

Poland's air, walked through its fields, worried about people hiding in barns. And whenever she read it she felt remorse—the kind you feel when someone has died and you realize that you've never paid enough attention to them. She thought of the times she'd listened to her husband with half an ear and of the times he asked where he put his glasses and car keys and she hadn't helped him look. After a while, she began to have similar feelings about Poland—a country she'd never paid attention to. She studied its maps, went to Polish movies, bought a book of Polish folk songs. Poland stayed on her mind like a small, subliminal itch.

One day when she was driving on a back-country road, she looked in her rear-view mirror and saw Poland in back of her. It was snowy and dark, the Poland of her husband's poem. She made turns, went down other roads, and still it was there, a country she could walk to. It was all she could do to keep from going there, and when she came home she mailed the poem to her husband's first wife, explaining it was the last thing he'd ever written and maybe she'd like to have it. It was a risky thing to do—neither liked the other—and in a matter of days she got a call from the woman who said: *Why are you doing this to me, Ellen? Why in God's name don't you let me leave him behind?* There was static on the line, a great subterranean undertow, and soon both women were pulled there, walking in the country of Poland. He was there, too, always in the distance, and the first wife, sensing this, said, "Well, as far as I'm concerned, he can just go to hell." She said this almost pleasantly—it wasn't an expression of malice—and the second wife answered: "I agree. Completely. It's the only way."

LANDING STRIP

ON THE WAY TO PAINT THE LANDING STRIP, THE soldiers could talk only of the bombing in Baghdad that morning. A whole street of shops, one shop after another, the last shop being the most expensive perfume shop in Baghdad. Hundreds of perfumes in glass bottles. Colognes. Bath salts. Soaps. Vapors so sweet you wanted to hold your nose.

The bombing had happened minutes before the perfumer came to open up in the morning. A pompous little man in his thirties who had inherited the business from his father. An hour later one of the soldiers had arrived and the perfumer was running around his bombed-out shop, pulling out Oriental rugs, mopping any small surface he could find—he meant to capture the smells forever. They had to drag him away.

It was night as they drove to the desert. Their job was simple: to paint a landing strip black, making sure the edges were jagged so it looked like a bombed-out crater. When they got to the landing strip they rigged up some lights, concealed them with a canopy of parachute silk. They poured black paint over the strip and began to spread it with huge rollers. The solider who had been to the perfumer's shop wouldn't join in. He had a different idea about how to do the job. Namely in the dark, because it was safer.

The canopy wasn't large. After painting six or seven feet of the landing strip, they had to move the canopy, along with paint cans, brushes, lights. The silk rustled, the ceiling sagged, the enormous vats sloshed paint. The soldier who had been to Baghdad stood in the sand cracking jokes; but around three in the morning he persuaded them to dismantle the canopy and lights. "Let me finish in the dark," he said.

"Fine with us," said the others. They lay in the sand, smoked cigarettes, gossiped. Again the talk turned to the perfumer's shop. "A pompous little man," said the soldier who was painting. "When they managed to pull him away he had all these little pieces of cloth, saturated with different perfumes. Makes me almost happy for the bombing." "Oh?" called one of the soldiers in the sand. "And why do you say that?" "Because he was an ass, that's why. Running around like he could save things. It doesn't matter anyway. He'll build himself another shop in no time."

The soldier on the sand got up and punched the soldier who was painting. Vats spilled. A helmet cracked. The others rushed in, pulled them apart, brought out the parachute silk, rigged up the canopy and lights. They painted through the night, not saying a word, except once, near dawn, when someone said:

"When the war is over, we should paint his whole shop black, don't you think? And those damned perfume bottles, too, while we're at it!"

BUYING A RUG IN ESQUARES

AT SEVEN-THIRTY IN THE MORNING A MAN NAMED Arthur Moldera from the United States knocked on the door of a famous rug weaver in Esquares, Mexico. Her name was Asunta Martinez, he had seen her once before on a visit to Esquares several years ago with his wife. She had led them into her workroom, asked them about a design, and the two of them had argued so violently about the kind of rug they wanted that she sent them away, saying, "I can't deal with the two of you, come back when you agree. You Americans," she shouted after them, as they walked down the street, "you put these rugs on your walls, not on your backs or your floors. How in the world can you agree on a design?" She made herself a brew of strong black tea, and went back to her loom.

―――――

To Arthur's relief, the rug weaver didn't recognize him. After sizing him up, she led him, once again, into her small interior workroom, piled with rugs, knickknacks, crucifixes. Arthur sat still, his elbows close, but when he took out the design of the rug he wanted—the same design he and his wife fought over four years ago—he managed to knock over a small wooden bird perched on the shelf right next to him. The rug weaver waved away his apologies, then looked at the design. "Pretend folk art," she said, pointing to the stylized black flowers and a light blue stiletto shoe in the upper right hand corner. She concentrated on the shoe: "This is blasphemous. Do you really want it in the rug?" "Yes," said Arthur, nodding. He was an architect and had designed the rug himself, although he didn't mention this. She looked at his sketch carefully, clearly not remembering it, then quoted Arthur a price which he knew to be outrageous. "A month," she said. "I'll finish it in a month."

<hr>

As soon as the deal was made, Arthur felt a wave of relief. He walked back to his hotel, called his answering machine, checked his messages. Not surprisingly there was a message from his ex-wife, who sensed his departures like radar. Hello, I'm in town, thought I might see you. Her voice was indifferent, curious. Also a message from his girlfriend. How's the weather in Mexico? Arthur scribbled her a note, then thought of writing

Leah. Guess what? I'm finally getting the rug. He didn't.

After he and Leah had gotten divorced, Arthur had knocked about in their old, empty Victorian for nearly a year, moving his sleeping bag from room to room. One night, in the living room, he'd had a vision of the rug where it always belonged, right above the fireplace. Arthur had never had a vision. It was Leah who ran to psychics, conferring about auras, past lives, future prospects. But here was the rug—*his* rug—hovering over the fireplace with numinous authority. It was about midnight. Arthur could hear two people arguing on the street. Without remembering that most of his things were in boxes, Arthur crawled out of his sleeping bag and began to look for the design of the rug in the drawers of an empty desk. When he didn't find it there, he progressed to orange crates. At three in the morning he found the design in a box labeled *Trips*, wedged between a brochure on Puerto Villarta and a picture of Leah on the beach. The picture was face up, inviting him to look. Pale blond, artfully disheveled hair, pale blue eyes, a face that looked slightly sketched.

Now Leah lived in a town on the coast where it always rained. She was an interior decorator, sounded happy. Arthur looked out the window of his room, and saw a white donkey nibbling on rose petals. The last time they'd been here, Leah had worried about the animals eating flowers. "Do you think they're hungry?" she'd asked more than once.

That night, in the courtyard of his hotel, Arthur met a man named Estevan with the same last name as his. There was little chance that they were related: Arthur's family had come to the States from Spain. Estevan's family had been in Mexico for three generations. Nonetheless, the common name fueled the sense of a bond and in the lush, dense courtyard, filled with bougainvillea and night-blooming jasmine, they told each other stories, first of childhood, then of marriage, one in Arthur's case, two in Estevan's. Arthur told Estevan about his vision of the rug—the same rug he and Leah had fought over five years ago, in front of Asunta Martinez, who had sent them away, shouting after them, "I'm not a priest! I don't settle disputes!" Arthur was a restrained man. Yet as he talked, he became emotional and foreign, as if his voice were molded from the hot, thick night. His Spanish waxed eloquent, he said poetic things. Soon he told Estevan what he'd only dreamed—that getting this rug felt like a redemption, the beginning of a new life. When he was finished, Estevan sighed and wished him well. Then—as if he knew he were treading on something delicate—he said:

"Just one thing. Maybe you should be careful about this Asunta Martinez. A friend of mine came all the way from Vera Cruz to get her to make a rug, and he got taken for a ride, at least that's what he said." "How?" "Well, of course, I don't know. But he said she wove in pornographic figures so skillfully, they looked like flowers until he put the rug up on his wall. You can't imagine what he saw. Or said he saw: The most obscene stuff. Animals and children. Women and birds. He's not naive, but he was so upset he wrapped the rug around two stones and threw it in a pond." "Do you believe him?" "Oh, yes! Otherwise I wouldn't be telling you. Anyway, Oxaca is famous for rugs. Why don't you go there to get what you want?"

⸻

After Estevan left, Arthur stayed on in the courtyard, smelling the night-blooming jasmine, drinking wine, looking for signs, talismans. Estevan's story dissolved the apparition of the rug, shrunk it from a vision to a random dream. I should never have talked, Arthur thought, and this thought—his first thought that evening in plain English—felt cold and real.

Later, he walked all the way to the edge of town, stood on his toes to look in the window of the rug weaver's workroom. In the moonlight, he saw all kinds of rugs—rugs stacked on the floor, the wall, spilling out of sturdy wooden trucks. He tried to imagine men and women tangled in strange poses, children and animals copulating. But he couldn't see them, and now he regretted the whimsical high-heeled shoe he'd wanted in the upper right hand corner. He decided to write the rug weaver a note and ask her not to use it.

While he was looking for paper, Arthur saw a mound stir in the alcove off the workroom. It rose and moved toward the door. "What are you doing in front of my grandmother's house?" said a man's voice, pursuing Arthur as he hurried down the street. "Don't you know you can't come here except by appointment?" "I was just about to make one," said Arthur. "I need to discuss a rug. I want to change part of the design." The man, who was taller than Arthur, looked blank. Arthur took a pad from his shirt pocket and wrote his name on it, adding *cliento*. "Will you give this to the rug weaver?" he asked. "Tell her I'll come by again later in the morning." The man shrugged, took the paper, and walked away. Suddenly he turned around and shouted: "Voyeur! Pervert! I won't be your messenger at all!" Shutters opened, doors slammed, and Asunta Martinez walked down the street, looking regal in a maroon flannel bathrobe and enormous slippers. When she came to Arthur she spoke in perfect English.

"I remember you," she said. "You're the gentleman with the very loud wife. And here you are, arguing again! You wanted a rug with a shoe in the corner? Okay, you'll get a rug with a shoe in the corner. But you're still arguing, aren't you? You and your shitty rug." More shutters had opened. Arthur waited, expecting a banishment. But all she said was: "The rug will be ready tomorrow. Is that good enough? If it's ready tomorrow will you leave?" "Yes," Arthur said, forgetting to mention the shoe.

=====

"How wonderful," said Arthur's girlfriend, Olga, when he told her he was coming back the next evening. "You'll be home. And you'll have your rug!" While they talked—he could hear a scraping sound over the phone. "What are you doing? filing your nails?" "No," said Olga. "Pumice stone. I'm in the bathtub."

=====

That night Arthur found Estevan Moldera in the courtyard drinking wine. "Guess what? She's making me the rug in a hurry. Like tomorrow." "Really?" "Yes. She wants me out of town." "Good." "Good?" "Yes," said Estevan. "Good." He seemed to have forgotten their conversation and looked like he wanted to be alone. Nonetheless, Arthur sat down. "Was that story true?" he asked. "What story?" "The story about the pornographic rug." "Yes, it was true. You think I would lie?" "Maybe. Is this a habit with her?" "I don't know. I just know it happened to my friend. Like I said." Yesterday Estevan had told Arthur that he'd come to Esquares to talk to his former wife about some shared property. He spoke as if this were commonplace, something he did often. Now Arthur looked at Estevan and imagined an enormous wooden door being slammed in his face, a large carved door one might call a portal. The interior of the house contained mysteries, possibly another man. "Can I do anything?" he said. "No. Nothing," said Estevan. "I'm tired." "I'm getting the rug made with the shoe," said Arthur, by way of sounding interesting. "What?" said Estevan. "The shoe," he said, "the light blue stiletto shoe in the upper right hand corner. She's weaving it for me, after all." "Good," said Estevan, as though Arthur had clarified something important. Arthur realized then that Estevan was drunk.

He went to his room, began to pack. Socks. Stamps. A guide book. Silver earrings for Olga. At one in the morning, he peered into the courtyard, saw Estevan at the wrought-iron table. "Would you like to go see Asunta Martinez?" he called. "Are you nuts?" Estevan answered. Arthur went down to the courtyard, sat down at Estevan's table. Estevan poured him a stingy amount of wine, told him the entire story: Indeed his ex-wife had been outraged when Estevan appeared and indeed she had slammed a large wooden door right in his face. Also another man had been inside, Estevan had seen him in the hallway. The fact that truth corresponded so perfectly with what Arthur had imagined reinstated his belief in miraculous one-to-one correspondences, restored his vision of the rug. "Come," he said, tugging at Estevan's sleeve. "Come, let's go see Asunta Martinez." At first Estevan was stubborn. "I won't creep through this god-awful town to see some silly old lady weaving a rug. I've already been a supplicant once today." "You're not a supplicant. You're a witness!" Estevan grumbled, got up, and the two men crept through the town, past the square, until they came to the rug weaver's house, where a light was on. She was alone, by herself, in half-light, head bent, fingers flying, working quickly, rapidly, alone. Arthur looked. His rug was half-done and looked perfect, not one optical illusion. She had already woven the shoe, and it didn't look blasphemous at all, but delicate, sacred, strange. Pale blue, almost white, just as he'd imagined it.

"How does she do it?" he asked, to Estevan, who had fallen asleep. "How does she do it?" he said to himself. He shook Estevan, and they walked back to the hotel, but not before he paused before the white donkey eating roses. "My wife loved this animal," he said, although he had no idea whether it was the same donkey Leah had seen five years ago. "She talked about him with great affection and always worried whether he got enough to eat."

Estevan nodded amiably, the way people nod when they are drunk.

ZELDA

MARLA AND I MET AT A CLINIC FOR THE MARGINALLY insane. We were doing internships in psychology and supposed to be setting an example. I wore a tie and clean blue jeans and Marla wore heels and her only suit. On the very first day, I noticed Marla, looking friable and on edge, and went over and asked what was going on. Within moments she was telling me how she hated the clinic and really wanted to be an artist. Her eyes were deep and her hoop earrings were large and her blouse was missing a button. After clinic hours we made love in the therapists' conference room with the door locked and our clothes on. Then we tried living together, but I found Marla's apartment too messy, even for me, with drawers spilling earrings and scarves and underwear and a kitchen table piled with laundry. Finally we agreed it had been a bond based on lust and loneliness. We managed to remain friends.

When we got our degrees, we moved into very different offices: I chose a modern building with excellent plumbing, and Marla and a group of friends were taken in by the charm of an old-world building.

The landlord knew the building was a relic and intended to keep it that way; but since Marla and her colleagues all wished they were living in Europe, they didn't complain when the plumbing went bad or rain drenched them during sessions. Even so, the landlord accused them of glutting the system with tampax so they bought a "special-needs" container for the bathroom. It was small and white with a pointed roof.

<hr />

One Saturday Marla knocked on my door and said she was going to quit being a therapist and go to an artist's colony in Oregon. The decision was a long time coming, but the catalyst was getting locked in the bathroom of her office with her landlord. "Two hours with that creep," she said. "You can't believe it."

No one had been around when the door jammed, and Marla had to beg someone on the street to phone the landlord. When he came, he wouldn't come upstairs, but talked to Marla from the street. He told her that the door was old and could easily break if he tried to jimmy it open from the outside. Marla told him she would die if she had to live in the bathroom.

"Finally," Marla said, "he got a ladder and came through the bathroom window and almost broke his balls on that pointed tampax box he made us buy. He brought hammers and screws and drills, but we were trapped. It got dark and people came to the office for evening sessions, but no one could use the bathroom. He kept chipping away at the lock, and between the chipping he talked to me about his back and a couple of knee-operations. Finally someone tapped on the door from the outside and it opened, just like that. When I left, people in the waiting room clapped and laughed like we'd given a performance. Therapists play God. They sit on high thrones. But it only took a minute to see how happy people are when one of us gets locked in a bathroom."

I was quiet and didn't argue. Marla asked for wine, then ran her hands through her hair and said: "I need to ask you a favor. I want you to take one of my clients. She's wonderful. Her name is Zelda. I can't pass her on to anybody else."

"Why not?"

"Because: Zelda is amazing. She sees people very clearly. In fact, when I told her I was quitting she said she'd seen it coming for weeks just by the way I looked out the window. She's the only one of my clients who has a soul."

"How can you legislate like that?" I said. "Everybody has a soul. No wonder you think we're high-handed." Marla didn't answer. The implication was: *Zelda's soul is important.*

Marla gave up her practice and went to the artist's colony in Oregon, and Zelda called the following week. On the phone her voice was soft, and when she came to see me she emanated order. "Why do you want to be in therapy at all?" I asked. "Just to talk," she answered. She then said she wanted to talk about Marla, not herself, because Marla had made an incredible change in her life, and she needed to understand it. I asked her why, and she said: "I'm simply interested."

Zelda was small and dark, and led a thoughtfully organized life, with dancing lessons every day and occasional performances. She was beautiful in the way children or dancers are beautiful, with an innocent, seamless face. She came once a week to talk about Marla, and every week I listened, trying, because it was my job, to find some hidden meaning. Zelda was very precise in the way she used language and the more she talked the more I began to have a sense of how the whole event had really looked. "Why do you think she was standing there?" I asked, when Zelda imagined Marla by the bathroom sink. "Because she didn't want to get too close to him, but she didn't want him to feel disliked." "And what do you think they really said?" I asked. "Did he only talk about himself, or did she talk, too?" "Oh, no, I'm sure Marla made a lot of jokes and kept saying she'd die if she had to live there. You know Marla, she does that."

I'd never thought about the fact that Marla's eyes, which are green, had remained green in the bathroom. Or that the landlord, who valued the aesthetic beauty of his building at all costs, might have been willing to stay there for days. The more Zelda talked, the more the whole event became a distinct, microcosmic journey, until one day Marla got small, like a speck of dust, and I said to Zelda: "Look, we aren't doing therapy. So there's no point in your paying me." Zelda agreed, and we began to meet at cafes.

—————

Meanwhile, Marla was sending me letters that justified her amazing turning-point brought about by a jammed bathroom lock. *I get up at five every morning and I paint and paint and paint until my cortex pops and then I paint some more,* she wrote in one letter. And in another: *The people here are great, and yesterday I had a kind of illumination just by looking at some rice in the kitchen; each grain was luminous.* When I read the letters, I envied her, but then I thought, no I'm too even-handed to give up therapy, and anyway, look what I'm doing with Zelda.

I told Zelda about the letters, and she was pleased. "Marla did the right thing," she said, handing me a bowl of green tea. "Yes," I said, "I guess she did." "No, really," Zelda emphasized. "She followed her lights." "Yes," I agreed, "she followed her lights." Our eyes flicked back and forth across the tea bowls. "Do you think I've followed my lights?" I asked. "I don't know. Maybe."

In a couple of months Marla began to sour about the artist's colony: *I can't believe that my disillusionment started in the bathroom again,* she wrote. *Maybe I didn't tell you that all the bathrooms here are very small and there aren't any locks on the doors and sometimes men and women are so spaced-out they pee in front of each other even though it isn't encouraged. I have no sense of privacy and now whenever I think about those two hours in the bathroom with that creep they seem pleasant and sometimes I wonder what I'm doing here.* For a moment I returned to my old therapist ways and began to wonder about Marla and bathrooms. But when I told Zelda she said it was expected: "Rooms create incredible turning-points for people. You know that."

Zelda and I had become lovers—something that seemed natural, based on her clarity of vision. We mostly lived in her apartment, which made me feel calm. Her dancing clothes were on hangers and her stamps and paper-clips were in jars and her collections of stones and coins were in wooden boxes. When we ordered Chinese food to-go, Zelda brought out real chopsticks. At one point I said to her, "What will we do if Marla comes back?" She looked undisturbed and said: "Well, we'll tell her."

One day I got an alarming letter from Marla: *I've decided that the life of an artist is also a crock and plenty of people here envy me for having a way to earn a living. So I'm coming back to do therapy, and I want you to let Zelda know she can resume with me if she wants to. Of course people have to try things and I've certain taken risks but I know when to cut my losses.*

Of course there was nothing to resume. I told Zelda about the letter and she said she didn't want to be in therapy anymore—and in any case, before she left, Marla had told her that therapy absorbed people into the culture and made them all the same. "I'll write and tell her that," said Zelda. "No, I will," I said. I wrote Marla a half-truth, saying that Zelda had discontinued treatment because she'd been so impressed by what Marla had said about therapy, and then I chided her for not living up to her principles. I was frightened of Marla's anger, so I added: *Believe me, Marla, I'm saying all this because I believe in you. I think you should stay in that colony and be an artist.*

———

Marla came back to town looking more blowsy than ever, and when she asked me about Zelda, I said Zelda had moved to a different city and was dancing in an avant garde troupe. "An avant garde troupe? But Zelda is classical." "Marla," I said, "she's changed."

It took Marla just about a month to find us in a cafe. "I can't believe it of either of you!" she shouted, peering down at our capucinoes. "You can both go to hell." Zelda looked unruffled. "It was all your influence," she said to Marla. "Really?" "Yes," said Zelda, "profoundly." I had a beer at the zinc bar and let them talk. I could see them in the mirror—Zelda looking patient, Marla growing calm. "I never really wanted you anyway," Marla said when I came back. To Zelda she said: "I always knew you had a soul."

That night Zelda sat cross-legged on her bed and looked at me solemnly. "Actually, I've been thinking of leaving town," she said. "There are better set-ups for dancers in other cities, and besides I think I want to go back into therapy and there's no one here I can talk to." "Why do you want to bother with therapy at all?" I asked. "Because," she said, "I think I have another angle." I never asked what the angle was, and I couldn't persuade her to stay. The week before Zelda left, I spent a lot of time looking at her face, wondering if I'd be able to remember it.

POSTCARDS

LONG BEFORE YOU DIED, YOU PROMISED TO SEND YOUR friends postcards from beyond the grave that said: *Having a wonderful time, wish you were here.* You said you would choose a conventional photograph of American scenic grandeur—and you would pre-address and stamp the postcards yourself.

This was in the early stages of your illness. I appreciated the sharpness of your mind, and your quote, from Johnson, that "there's nothing like the anticipation of the noose to strengthen a man's wit." I laughed, felt hopeful, said you wouldn't need to send the postcards for a long time. But after you told me I worried that you would ask me to mail them, and whenever you came to visit I thought you were bringing postcards. I could imagine scenes in which you asked me to mail them, and I said I wouldn't, and you got angry and eventually I said I would. But this never happened: All we ever did was sit around, make jokes and drink tea. Once you came over wearing a black top hat, black jeans and a black shirt and told me that your illness was about to get worse. I asked you how you knew and you said that always before entering a new stage, you had an impulse to change your hair, grow a moustache, buy off-beat clothes, use a cane—as though death might know your name but not your face.

━━━

As it turned out, the only thing you ever wanted from me was supreme restraint in leaving you alone when you began to die. You told most of your friends to go away and they did, and you also said no one could cry at your funeral, and we obeyed. You liked junk food, so your family served macaroni salad and salami and popcorn, and we all stood around pretending to have fun. I assumed you'd been too sick to remember the postcards, but a month after you died, I got one that said: *Having a wonderful time, wish you were here.* It was in your small, slanted handwriting and the words transmitted your voice. For a moment I could hear you speaking.

The postcard was a color photograph of American grandeur with mountains, sky, sea, and a meadow of flowers. When I look at it now, I remember what I used to imagine when I'd see you coming to my door: You asking me to mail the postcards. My saying no. A terrible explosion of anger. And then my saying yes. You open the palm of your hand. You offer me hundreds of postcards.

ANIMAL SKINS

A FEW WEEKS BEFORE SHE LEFT FOR THE MOUNTAINS, she said to him: Do you know that if I touch you in a certain way, you'll feel like a vole? They were in bed, reading. She put out her cigarette, touched him softly, and he felt he had silky fur. He'd never seen a vole, but had an instant understanding of different gradients of earth, just the way she understood layers of snow—depth-hoar, crystal-snow—he'd heard her talk about them. Then she stroked him with the back of her hand and he was racing along the ground. What was I then? he asked. You were a fox, she answered.

She was going to the mountains alone—that was the understanding. She was a professional skier, so the separation made sense. Still, there was tension surrounding her trip because she was going to ski in country that had avalanches. One night he read a book about mountain rescue, and realized that all the techniques required another person. He mentioned this and she said she wasn't afraid.

That evening he watched her pack and he had an insatiable desire to follow her. What animals will you see? he said. I have no way of knowing, she answered. He persisted, saying that he wanted her to touch him so he could become each animal on her journey. She said she didn't want to be bothered, and soon they had a fight in which she said his reading the book about mountain rescue was a form of meddling and he said he could read any damn book he pleased. She got into bed and began to smoke. The smoke reminded him of powder snow—the kind that can cause avalanches.

All that month he thought about her in the mountains, especially when he was in bed, trying to recreate the feeling of her hands. He thought about being an animal in snow, imagined her finding him, a moment of locked eyes.

As soon as she came back, he made her tell him every animal she'd seen. Foxes mostly, she said. And maybe a few deer. The usual. She was standing by the closet unpacking clothes, looking relaxed, a little smug. The animals I expected to see, she added.

He came over and gripped her by the shoulders —at a distance, so he could see her eyes. They were bright, as though they had seen acres of snow, great impossible bolts of it, traversing an entire country. He hesitated, then stroked her lightly, turning her into an animal he'd never seen. Who am I? she said. I have no idea, he answered. He carried her to the bed and put her under piles of blankets, an avalanche of sorts, far away from the mountains. Don't think about anything, he whispered, everything is known inside the skin.

SNOW

WHEN HE KNOCKED ON THE DOOR OF THE FUNERAL parlour, he had three questions, and these were distinct in his mind, just like the moment when he'd got the news. The door had a glass panel dusted with snow: He looked inside to see a hazy version of himself, which disappeared as the door was opened by a man in blue workclothes. "You family?" said the man. "In a way," said Errol. "I knew her before she moved back." "I see," said the man, leading Errol past an umbrella stand, which held two dry wreaths. And then, as if anticipating his first question, he said: "Well, at least she wasn't alone." They came to a sitting room which smelled like an attic, and the man stopped before a large oak door. "You're not family, are you?" he said.

Ryan lay in a small white room, looking deflated and a little bue. Waxen was the word, he supposed. She wore a light blue sweater, and the rest of her body was covered. "Her mother wanted it that way," said the man. "She wanted her to look real casual." He reached into his pocket for tobacco, and Errol remembered the rose in his side pocket. It was wrapped in waxed paper, and he could feel the cool, fragile head through the fabric.

"Was the other woman as frozen?" he asked. "Oh," said the man, "who knows? I mean, when you find two frozen ladies in the snow, the last thing you think is to compare them." He poured tobacco in his hand, threw the mound into his mouth, and began to chew.

These were his questions: Had Ryan been alone? Was the other woman as frozen as she was? Who had seen her last before the hike? Because he'd read the newspaper, he knew the answers, but he wanted to be told, as though hearing for the first time. He wanted the feeling of someone *giving* him the news, just as the woman at the coffee counter had *given* him the German rose: "Would you like a rose?" she said to him. "Yes," he answered. "It's a German rose," she said, handing him a red flower. "From Germany?" "No! Just a German rose. . . ."

As soon as the woman walked away, he carried the rose to a newspaper stand where he saw the headline: FROZEN HIKER REVIVES. Two women had frozen in the snow. Later, in a mountain cabin, one had come to life. Blood had warmed her veins. Spring had entered her body. But the other woman had died. "Oh, she melted okay," said the man who found them. "But she never got warm. Nothing I could do."

—————

Outside there was a sudden noise and cars sped through the ploughed streets like a flock of geese. One car stopped near the window. "Her mother," said the man, spitting out the tobacco.

"I know," said Errol, pretending to recognize the car. He snuck a look at Ryan again, remembering that nails and lashes continue to grow. They were like after-thoughts, or skidding wheels, and these images surprised him, because supposedly you couldn't think in metaphors when someone died: His friend Sylvia had told him that. "Was Peter Handke's account of his mother's suicide a *creative* venture?" she was asking her class when he'd stopped to say good-bye. "I mean wasn't it just a *report*?" She noticed Errol standing by the door and said, "Well, come in!" And then, when he didn't, she walked over to him and whispered: "Are you driving all the way? Well, if you are, be careful. . . ."

—————

Heels crunched on the ice, and Ryan's mother entered the room with red roses that matched her cummerbund. "Errol," she said, putting out a gloved hand, "we want people to remember Ryan as she was when she *lived,* not as she was when she *died.*" They shook hands; the snow on her glove changed to ice. She smiled, and her mouth changed from a poppy to two red leaves.

"Well, I've seen," Errol said, taking another look at the lashes.

Ryan's mother fussed with the flowers until they cascaded over the hill made by Ryan's feet. When she was finished, Errol offered her his rose, which nearly matched the others. "No, these are a gift from the bishop," she said. "You can put them over there." And she pointed to a jar of hyacinths on a flat exhibit case. Errol walked to the case, and attempted to arrange the rose: it stuck awkwardly above the heavy blue flowers.

The exhibit case was filled with pictures of Ryan: Ryan at three holding a ball. Ryan at twenty-six next to an abstract painting. Ryan with her new boyfriend, Marcus, touching a free-form sculpture. There was a local bar a few blocks from the Episcopal Church, and before the funeral he sat there drinking scotch, thinking about Ryan's paintings. For no particular reason, he remembered a gouache she'd done of old people sitting on the hoods of cars, and wondered whether Ryan's mother had considered putting it in the exhibit case. He guessed that she hated the painting, and he liked knowing that, just as he liked knowing that she was angry at him for looking at Ryan when she was dead. This impression was confirmed, because at the funeral she whispered something to an usher, who led him to a back pew: He didn't mind, because a woman he knew was there, and the one time he cried, she put her arms around him.

The second to the last time he'd seen Ryan, they'd taken a bath together: it wasn't quite dusk, and the sun made each water bubble fill with light; each light created a tiny star, tagging along in the water. "There's a big difference between memory and imagination," Ryan told him. And then she accused him of not listening. "Oh but I *am* listening," he said. "I am." The bubbles burst, the stars vanished; then new bubbles formed, all with new stars. "Memory is horizontal," said Ryan, "imagination is vertical." There had been a mirror across the room, and he had watched himself put his chin on Ryan's neck and stick a wet finger in her mouth. "Do you want to go inside?" he said.

In her bedroom they lay on the sheets like landlocked fish. "You have to wait," said Ryan, "it always takes me a while." He waited, Ryan fell asleep, and he crept out of bed to find several children's books in braille. He pressed his hands on the pages, imagining that one touch from his fingers brought the scenes to life. "What are you doing?" said Ryan when she woke up. "Why reading," he said, "just like your kids. . ."

A few days later he came by to pick Ryan up for dinner and found the door open, the house dark, and Ryan in a straight-backed chair reading braille. "The lights are out," she said, "because I don't want to cheat." And then she told him she was going back to Maine to teach in a school for the blind.

Ryan's students were at the funeral—blind children to whom she'd taught sculpture and braille. After the service, they sat in the church-social room like illumined presences, surrounded by kneeling adults who offered them cake. They seemed enclosed in the privilege of wisdom, so often associated with the blind. Only one of the children mentioned Ryan. She tugged at a teacher's skirt and asked: "Do we get to be there when she burns?"

It was seeing these children that had made him cry during the service. He had been gripped by the thought of Ryan doing something she would never do again. "I'm surprised she came back here to teach," said the woman who had held him. "I'm more surprised she won't do it anymore," he said. It then occurred to him that Ryan hadn't *wanted* to unfreeze. If she had wanted to, she would have—just like the other one. "Ryan froze and melted and burned, in that order," he said, "because she didn't like miracles." "Oh come on, Errol," said his friend, "nothing is that easy."

The woman who had been with Ryan in the snow sat in a corner looking humble, like a saint. One morning she had been a secretary in the school for the blind: The next evening she had become a Houdini of physiology, a woman performing feats with frozen blood. "How did I do it? I didn't. Just waking up in this rush of water . . . I've heard of people who died and came to life, seen them on television. And they always have this sense of awe, but I don't feel that, because I don't remember. . . ."

She spoke loudly, touching her silver earrings. People who knew her were convinced that the melting hadn't stopped with her body but had reached a frozen river in her brain. "She talks so much," said a woman in a flowered dress. "But so *articulate*," said a friend. Her parents sat by her like sentries, offering her cookies, and her fiancé (or so he was introduced) knelt to her right. When the cake was brought (it was a *bûche de Noël* that looked remarkably like a snowbank), the unfrozen woman rushed over to Errol with a large slice. "I feel I've known you," she said. "My name is Kate."

———

That night, when the streets were brightly lit, Errol walked to Ryan's house. The sky was a rich black and the snowbanks were piled so high the streets felt like a maze. The house, lit and humming with the attendants who surround the dead, was easy to find. Ryan's brother was in the living room, stacking paintings. Two women were in the bedroom sorting clothes. And Marcus, Ryan's new boyfriend, was in the kitchen playing cards with Kate, who was wearing one of Ryan's hats. Errol ignored them and walked to Ryan's studio. Nothing on the walls. A few chairs conversing with the night. And, on the floor, some boxes with things for collage—stuff from the sand and sea, stuff from attics and dimestores. Behind one box, Errol found a painting of a blue sky filled with white clouds. High in the sky, Ryan had pasted a photograph of two manicured hands. Where the thumbs and forefingers met, she had attached piece of string, so it looked as though the hands were offering the string from the sky: he was reminded of the gesture of the rose, and began to search for wrapping paper, when Kate appeared at the door. She was still wearing Ryan's hat, and he was holding the picture of the hands—they were almost as large as his own. He didn't want anybody to know he was taking the picture, but he had no choice, so he showed it to Kate who said Yes, she had always liked Ryan's art, and wasn't it strange that he had found this—almost as though. . . . "Yes," he said, "almost as though the hands were meant for me." "That's exactly what I mean." And then she said how strange it was that the snow had frozen them: if only they'd been thinking, they could have crawled into a snowbank, and stayed there until help came. "Yes," Errol said. "The snow is like that: it can make you warm or cold." He wanted to ask Kate questions, questions he didn't know the answers to, but nothing occurred to him, so he let her talk on, comforting himself with the thought of the two women in a snowbank—huddled there like bears, on friendly terms with the dark.

A GIFT OF PAPER

AFTER HER HUSBAND DIED, SHE BEGAN TO GO TO CAFES and write him letters. She had no sense that the letters would reveal anything important, she just wanted to make a gesture. She wrote descriptions of the cafes and told him things about her past and one day she wrote about a man sitting next to her in a grey, ill-fitting suit with a close, carefully trimmed beard. She wrote that he seemed apologetic and probably had given too many things to too many people. She also wrote that his beard was too carefully trimmed—a considered bastion against getting old. When she was done writing she got up and said good-bye, noticing that the man seemed disappointed that she hadn't asked him any questions. She went back to the same cafe, but she never saw him again. Soon after that she stopped writing letters to her husband.

A few years later, she saw the man at a party and their eyes met over a room of people. He walked over to her and said: "You wrote about me that day. What an invasion of privacy!"

She looked at him carefully. His beard was gone

and he didn't look that kind. "Yes," she said, "but it was only a diversion. "Well fuck you," he said, "for using me like an artist's model and not even asking my name." Then he left the party.

That night she went home and fished in the bottom of a drawer until she found the folder with letters to her husband. Their contents surprised her: One of the letters said that their marriage had been like a net, holding her from the open sea. Another said that she'd thought of leaving him long before he died, but her unhappiness felt so finely-tuned, she was afraid she would ruin some elemental force and fall apart. Finally she found descriptions of the man in the cafe. She had given him the fictional name of Ray de Groat and when she re-read what she had written, she found everything cruel and uncharitable. Among other things, she'd written a lie, which was that Ray de Groat had offered her paper from his briefcase because he wanted her to write in front of him the way other men might want a woman to undress. That night she burned all the things from the folder, and the next day went back to the same cafe. She'd hoped to see the man and apologize, but he wasn't there, so she decided she would write him a letter, then get his name and address from the hostess of the party; but she couldn't think of anything to say, so she put down her pen and stared out the window. It was raining and a florist was pulling in flowers from the rain. The florist worked under an awning near the cafe and had flowers on the sidewalk in silver pails. There were violets and roses and hydrangeas, and the florist pulled them in carefully, as if they were going on an unsettling journey, and the slightest disturbance would hurt their feelings.

SOULMATES

THE FIRST TIME I HEARD IT WAS IMPOSSIBLE TO LIVE with a soulmate was from my friend Marge who was three years older than me. She was sitting on her bed painting her toe-nails and I was sitting in a rocking chair watching her. Suddenly out of the blue, Marge said: "You can never live with a soulmate, it doesn't work. I've lived with three guys and I had too much in common with all of them. Believe me, the next guy I meet isn't going to like poetry, or Bach, or rainy mornings. We're going to meet pragmatically, and discuss what food we're going to buy and how we're going to raise the kids. Marriage isn't communication. It's *living*."

I'd never lived with a man and I couldn't stand what she was saying. I decided that she was being bitter because she'd lived with three guys and none of them had worked. She's deluded, I thought, and trying to spoil things for me. I reached for the polish and painted my toes. An extravagant earth-colored bronze.

Then it was 1982 and I was living with a man named Harlan Green. Harlan and I were soulmates: we had met in Paris, at a summer course for Americans at the Sorbonne. Eventually Harlan was going to go to medical school, but then he was nineteen and it turned out that we liked Yeats and a French poet named Supervielle. (We were always quoting a certain poem that began "O! old house of the light and rose!") We also agreed that beverages influenced one's sense of time: tea, for example, created a sense of leisure, while coffee created a sense of urgency. And over espresso on the Boulevard Saint-Michel, we agreed that the reason people got so crazy around Christmas was that they ignored the solstice, and just when they should be allowing themselves to be pulled into that primal sense of darkness they spaced-out at the peak of consumerism. After we came back to the States we decided to live together and the first thing we did was get a dog whom we named after Kafka's favorite sister. There had never been one doubt between us about the dog's name. We just looked at her when we saw her at the pound and thought: Ottla.

Fortunately, I had the restraint and presence of mind not to brag to Marge that I'd found a soulmate I could live with. She'd kept her word and was married to a lawyer with an excellent sense of humor.

Every week they planned their menus in advance, and he had already taught her how to rock climb. "It isn't Yeats," she wrote, "but it's a hell of a lot better than what I was getting."

⸻

One night, near Christmas, Harlan and I were in bed, talking. The bedroom was furnished according to our tastes: one simple oak dresser from the Salvation Army, an orange-plant by the window, a blue and white patchwork quilt, and a bedside table with a pitcher and a dark wooden bowl of winter pears. We were talking about the Crusades, when suddenly a great wind rose up from the trees. It was a wild, unruly wind, and seemed to be blowing in a perilous direction. I said this phrase *perilous direction* to Harlan, and he said, almost for the first time: "I don't know what you mean." "You don't know what I mean?" I said. "No," he said, "I really don't know what you mean." I paused and took a deep breath. Then I told Harlan something I'd never told anybody: namely, that ever since I've been a kid, I've always felt that the wind created a kind of time-warp so you could see things from other centuries. "If you listen," I said, "you can really see things beyond this time. You can literally be transported in some astral way." "I'm sorry," Harlan said. "I still don't know what you mean."

I remember the room very vividly then. Everything poised, wrapped inside the wind, the perfect furniture, the orange tree, all attuned to some higher frequency. "This feeling about the wind is important to me," I said, "something I've never told anybody." For a moment Harlan looked blank. Then he said: "Well, for me the wind is connected to the most awful night of my life, which is the night when my father walked out on my mother." He got out of bed, began to pace back and forth, and told me that one windy night in August he and his brother had to sit in his room listening to the most awful argument between his father and mother until his father slammed the front door and drove off. The next day he'd come back, bringing the boys a bunch of soap from the YMCA where he'd slept, but that night he and his brother didn't know if he was ever coming back, and they had to listen to the wind, and think that maybe their father had drowned, like the father of a classmate who had come home, stood outside the door, whistled his characteristic whistle, and then disappeared. The next day they'd found him in the river.

I listened to Harlan restlessly. I know I should care about what he was saying, yet I felt a distinct sense of claustrophobia. "I can't listen anymore," I said, "I just want to let the wind blow through my bones." Harlan scowled. I went out to our porch and stood there in my bathrobe. It was a violent wind. It was making garbage cans rattle, and blowing paper boxes and newspapers, sweeping them out of the world. I stood on the porch in my bathrobe, assuming a pose of enjoyment, but the truth was, I couldn't, because Harlan had made the wind sinister. Instead of messages from far-off places and esoteric times it was full of fathers sleeping at the Y or drowning. I went back inside, feeling cheated, and a little guilty, and meanwhile Harlan, in just a T-shirt with his hairy legs sticking out, was making tea. He looked sad, and drank his tea quickly, as though he really wanted it to be coffee.

"I wish you hadn't brought it up," he said. "This whole business about the wind. . . . It's really gotten to me. That was the most terrible night of my life."

"I'm sorry, Harlan. I was only talking about what the wind meant to *me*. It's been very influential. It's affected my way of life."

Harlan got up and put the tea cup in the sink. He took the tea bag from the cup and swung it like an pendulum. "Isn't that a little grandiose?" he said. "Pinning a major influence on one of the four elements? You're making yourself out like Black Elk or something."

"Well isn't it the same for you?" I asked. "Doesn't the wind have to do with the night your dad left?"

"That's different," he said. "It was just connected to something that happened to me by accident. But I'm not making out like it's special, or I have some transcendental connection to it."

Harlan said this peaceably, yet suddenly he

looked quite ornery in his T-shirt with the hair on his legs like spikes. "Screw you," I said. "You've really spoiled something." I went back to bed and listened to the wind, feeling hurt and still guilty, but thrilled again by its wildness. It was a dangerous wind. A perilous wind. I didn't care what Harlan said—it spoke to me.

As it turned out, it was one of the most violent winds that ever hit Northern California. It reached a velocity close to that of a tornado, and tore open the roof of a downtown department store called Hinks (which has since gone defunct and been made into seven movie theaters), and lifted up a lot of merchandise which landed on people's lawns. Our neighbor got a pin-ball machine and someone down the block got fifteen extension cords, and someone a block away got Christmas-tree ornaments. The next morning, which happened to be the morning of the solstice, everybody on our block was running around looking for things, and right on our front lawn, Harlan and I spotted two gnome-like figurines, an imitation crystal candle-holder, a pocket dictionary and a can of tennis balls. We were feeling angry and greedy, so we ran like mad and each of us got what the other didn't get his hands on. Then we looked at each other and knew we wouldn't be living together anymore.

Afterwards, there was the nagging question of whether I should tell Marge that she was right—it wasn't possible to live with a soulmate after all. She was divorced from the lawyer and living in Oregon, and the whole thing probably wouldn't have mattered to her; but somehow I felt that telling her would make her theory official. So I didn't. I kept it to myself.

Harlan moved from the apartment, leaving me with everything but the orange tree and the wooden bowl. Eventually I decided I needed more furniture, and got an oversized couch and a desk which made the place look like a student's apartment instead of a farmhouse in the south of France. That was seven years ago, and Harlan and I have remained friends. We don't see each other often, but always when we break up with someone, we call each other with a gloomy "Hello," and there's a feeling of being a soldier called back into the reserves. Just the other day I got such a call from Harlan. "Can I come over?" he said. "I'm really depressed." He had just broken up with a blond anesthesiologist who liked to windsurf—definitely not a soulmate. "Sure," I said, and he came right over from the hospital where he's doing his residency in interal medicine. His melancholy made him look vulnerable and when I noticed his stethoscope dangling from the pocket of his jeans, I felt jealous at the thought of him putting it close to other hearts. To make us both feel better, I told him Marge's old theory about soulmates, and he looked startled and a little angry. "For Godssake, why didn't you ever tell me before?" he said. "Think about the time we'd have saved."

"Do you think it was wasted time?" I said.

"Sure, in a way."

"But it was wonderful being with you."

"Really?"

"Oh yes. I wouldn't have not done it for the world."

Harlan was getting sleepy in a way that was familiar. We sat on my overstuffed couch, not quite touching, and it seemed, for a moment, that we were still the people who'd met in Paris, walking down those cobblestoned streets. I pressed my hand in his palm, he pressed back, and then his eyes seized on the figurine gnomes, and the candle-stick I've kept on the mantlepiece since I found them the day of the solstice. "You still have those?" he asked.

"Why yes," I said, "didn't you keep the dictionary and the tennis balls?"

"God, no. I lost the tennis balls and the dictionary was useless."

"Really? I'm surprised. They were kind of significant to me."

The pleasant, sleepy atmosphere turned to silence. I could see nubbly pieces of fabric on the couch, some of which were darker than the original beige. I picked one off and began to roll it in my hands..

"It's that wind," Harlan said. "Now whenever there's a wind I don't just remember my father—I remember that lousy night. Do you?"

"No. I love the wind. It reminds me of other centuries."

"Even after what happened?"

"Yes."

We looked at each other with the ill-will we'd discovered that night. "Your friend Marge is right," Harlan said. "Soulmates can't live together, after all. I think we should write some kind of confession and save other people time."

"For God's sake, Harlan. Let's not!"

"Why? Let the whole thing out in the open." He reached for a pencil on the coffee table and scribbled on the back of an envelope *forget about shared sensibilities.* "I'm going to make a list of every crazy assumption I've ever had about love," he said, "and then I'm going to refute it." "You're just angry," I said. "You're angry about breaking up with that blond." He didn't answer, kept on writing. I went into the bedroom, and called Marge in Oregon.

I hadn't spoken to Marge in ages, not since her divorce. When I called she was alone, working on a software project. She sounded gentle, sad and far-away. "I'm sorry," she said after I told her. "I didn't want to be right, and the opposite didn't work either. There's not any kind of theory about what kind of person you can live with."

I told her about Harlan wanting to publish a confession and asked her what she thought.

"Don't let him," she said. "At the very least people should find out for themselves. . . . Anyway, who knows? Maybe you *can* live with a soulmate."

We talked for a long while, said we'd try to see each other at Thanksgiving. When we hung up I went back to the living room and looked at the figurine gnomes. They were glazed with a bright green glaze and I could see parts of the room in them. Behind me, on the couch, Harlan had stopped writing and was staring at the ceiling. I sat next to him and stroked his hand.

"What do you think?" I asked. "Could soulmates live together?"

"Who knows?" said Harlan. "Maybe they could." And for a moment there was a flicker of static between us, like matches being struck.

MS. PACMAN

THERE WAS A TIME WHEN MY HUSBAND WOULD CALL ME from public telephones and ask: "Where am I? Can you guess?" Then I would guess where he was and if I guessed right, he would have to give me something and if I guessed wrong, I would have to give him something. He usually gave me flowers—although I hardly ever guessed right—and I usually gave him postage stamps. I didn't like this game. It gave me the feeling that Walker was thinking about moving out—which in fact he was. He never called me from very interesting places—usually telephone booths on ordinary streets in San Francisco, or, if our son Seth happened to be with him, from a video arcade where Seth played Ms. Pacman. Seth was only four and much too little to play the game well, but he loved seeing Ms. Pacman getting eaten up by light. If Walker had kept giving him quarters, Seth would have played again and again. Seth often said that he wanted to meet Ms. Pacman, and that he was in love with her. "How could you be in love with her?" I sometimes asked. "Because she's so brave," he always answered.

A few times I did guess where Walker was. But never by design, only by happenstance. "Did you know?" he would always ask. "Was it a *certain* guess?" "Oh leave me alone, Walker," I'd say. Sometimes I'd look in on phone booths, trying to get a sense of where people usually called from. A high-percentage called from outside drugstores, tapping their feet and writing lists. I never imagined Walker this way. I always saw him in that moment after dialing the phone, a kind of lost time, when one is poised, waiting. Once, when an errand for graphics-supplies brought me to the part of San Francisco near the bay, I did see him but not in a phone booth. He was leaving a discount dry-goods far from where he worked—it was on one of those wide prairie-streets near the Bay. "I've gotten material for sleeping bags!" he said. And then, as though it were the most common thing in the world for us to meet during the day, he took my arm and began to talk about Nepal. He said he wanted to go on a trek there. He said he wanted to mingle with the people. Presumably the sleeping bags were linked to this trip, but I was pretty sure he didn't mean for me and Seth to go with him. The next time he called and told me to guess where he was, I said: "You're in Nepal," to which he answered, "No, I'd never find a way to get there."

Walker's a cartographer. He's always told me that maps are the only romantic literature of the twentieth-century, and now he began to read them in the evening. Once Seth climbed on his lap and asked: "Where's the North Pole? Do they have penguins there?" "No," said Walker, pointing to a page on the atlas, "that's the South Pole. Would you like to go?" "Yes," said Seth, nodding his head. "Then we will," said Walker, not looking at me, and not adding the condition "some day." Seth looked at me and then turned to look at Walker. "Will we *all* go?" he asked. "All of us who want to," Walker answered.

———

"Are fish fierce?"

"Do geese eat fruit?"

"Are whales naked when they dive under the water?"

"Do coyotes eat fish?"

"Do lions eat ivy?"

"Do cats have feathers in their tails?"

"How do porcupines go to the bathroom with all their prickles?"

—these were the kinds of questions that Seth had begun to ask. They were almost always about animals, and often tinged with anxiety: I was sure that he was picking up Walker's thoughts about moving out—never stated, but in the air like an infection—and I kept waiting for the real question from Seth, the hard one. But this question never came, only more questions about animals

"Do monkeys eat pears?"

"Do crows dream?"

"Do owls like goats?"

"Can rabbits remember their mothers?"

———

Finally one night, when I was tucking him into bed, I asked:

"Seth, are you worried about anything? Is anything bothering you?"

"No," said Seth, turning away to look at his wall which we'd covered with luminescent stars.

"Are you sure?" I asked. "Would you talk to me if you were?"

"I don't know," said Seth. "Maybe." He kept looking at his wall and then suddenly he asked: "Do dwarfs come in different colors?"

"Dwarfs are the same as us," I said, "except they don't grow to be as big: they're the colors all people are."

"Am I a dwarf?"

"No. You're a kid."

"How about Ms. Pacman?"

"No, she's not a real person."

"How come?" said Seth. And then, before I could answer, he asked: "Are the kittens dwarfs?"

"No," I said, "they're tiny now, but they're

going to get big, like Elspeth."

As we talked, I could hear the kittens running all over the house. Our cat Elspeth had had them unexpectedly, at the age of eleven months, and now there were seven of them. They had begun to jump from high places, and whenever they landed on the rug, there was a soft thudding sound, like fruit falling from a tree. I heard this now, in the living room.

"Can I keep one?" Seth asked.

"Maybe."

That night after Seth went to sleep, Walker called at about nine-thirty and said:

"Okay—where am I?"

"Let's see," I said, listening to what sounded like cars. "You're somewhere outside—but not near your office. . . ."

"Right. But where?"

"Let's see . . . you're at a pay phone on Bay Street."

"No. Guess again."

"You're at a Pay N Save buying shampoo."

"No."

"I can't guess—I give up."

"I'm nowhere," said Walker, "I've pushed myself off the earth." He sounded tired and a little disoriented.

"Are you drunk?"

"No, I've just pushed myself off the globe, that's all. The world is flat and I was lucky enough to fall off it."

"Listen, Walker," I said, "what are you doing? What's going on?"

"Nothing," said Walker. "I'm just calling to ask you where I am. I'm giving you the chance to guess."

"Why?"

"Because I want you to. I want you to know."

"What do you want me to know?"

"Just where I am. It's important."

"Well I don't know. I've given up."

"Well I'll tell you then, I'm around the corner. I'm coming home."

"Walker, I'm tired."

"Do you want me to bring ice cream?"

"No."

═══════

By the time I posted ads for the kittens, Walker had started to collect boxes. I could see that he was thinking about moving out gradually—maybe even starting with a harmless-looking garage sale, the way he had done before Seth was born. He put the boxes in the garage, and Seth began to shift his focus from animals to disasters. He wanted to know what would happen when you put water on a volcano, and what he should do with his toys during an earthquake. Then he got sticks and began to create an arsenal in case of war.

"Are you sure you're not worried about something?" I asked.

"Yes," said Seth, who was trained to resist interrogation.

Seth had been with Walker on the most recent phone call. Walker had said he was in Bulgaria and then had dared me to guess where he really was. I hadn't been able to and Walker hadn't told me. Now I asked Seth, who said, without hesitation:

"In the arcade with Ms. Pacman."

People came to look at the kittens and one by one, in Seth's presence, they went away, to new homes, wrapped in towels or hidden in boxes, with a gift of catfood tucked away in the pockets of the new owners. I had told Seth that we could keep one kitten, and he had chosen a fluffy black-and-white cat who looked incongruously elegant. By now there were only three kittens in the house, tiny but intrusive presences, following us like ghosts, blending with the creaks and groanings of the house at night.

"Let's keep all of them," said Walker one evening, when he was sitting in his usual chair, reading by his usual light. He said this as if nothing were going to happen, as if there were no cardboard boxes in the garage.

"You mean the kittens?" I said.

"Sure," said Walker. "It's not like we're going to have more kids or anything."

"Walker," I said, "You have a lot of boxes in the garage. What's going on with you?"

There was a tense moment while Walker thought. Then he said: "Nothing, nothing at all."

"I think you have a girlfriend," I said, taking a plunge so he would tell me something.

"I have nothing of the kind." Then he said, "I have an itch. I want to go to Nepal."

"Alone?"

"I'm not sure. Anyway, it's just a thought." He frowned and went back to his map. It was made of rice-paper and so delicate, I could see his blue jeans through it. There were markings on the map, made firmly with a ballpoint pen.

"Is that Nepal?" I asked, going over to look at the map.

"No, it's Northern China."

I paused, sensing that this was a moment to ask, a time when things might be reversed. But all I said was, "I wish you'd talk to me." "Don't I?" Walker said, looking up.

His name was Eric Arbucci, and the minute I saw him I had the odd sensation that Walker had already left and I had invited a stranger over for coffee. He was shorter than I was, and wearing an apricot-colored shirt and a brown sports jacket. He wasn't my type, and I was pretty sure he was gay—but this didn't alter the sensation. He walked into the house and looked at the living room and smiled.

"I like this place!" he said. "I like all this white and the way you painted the fireplace!"

He was the kind of person who talked with exclamation points, but I didn't mind, I liked it. "Here they are," I said, bringing him over to the kittens, "have a look."

When he'd called about the kittens, and I'd told him they were only eight weeks old, he'd said: "My God they're young! Do they have fur yet?"

"Of course they do," I answered. "Haven't you ever had a cat?"

"Yes, but never a kitten. Oh, listen, what am I saying—cats always have fur, right?" He cupped his hand over the phone and yelled: "Hey Barry—do you want an orange tiger kitten?"

"Actually, I'd like two," a muffled voice yelled back.

"Hey," I said to him. "Where do you live? Who are you?"

"I live up in the hills," he said, "past Cragmont. Believe me, I'm an honorable man."

Now he knelt down by the tiger kitten who was

near the fireplace. "Oh, I like you," he said. "I want to take you home."

"Are you really honorable?" I asked.

"Absolutely. You can come over and see my house sometime."

I had promised Seth that I would let him say good-bye to all the cats when they left, so I woke him up, and he came into the living room looking sleepy. He kissed the orange tiger, and asked Eric if he'd send some pictures.

"Of course," said Eric. "You can even come to visit."

I gave Eric my usual complimentary package of litter and two cans of cat food, and the two of us walked to his car. He told me, in a rush, that he was a documentary film-maker who had moved from Los Angeles to be with his lover who taught French at the university. He said that his lover was a great cook, and then he told me that the moment we met he had the feeling we could be friends. He'd a vision of me, he said, sitting on their patio, while Barry was making enchiladas. "I think you're something else!" he said. "I hope I can get to know you."

I didn't say anything, and he said to me:

"What are you thinking?"

"I'm thinking that I'm married."

"That's strange. I had the oddest feeling that you weren't. Or am I wrong?"

"I don't know. My husband might be going to

Nepal. He's put some of his books in boxes, but he did that once before." I was about to tell him more—about how Walker had left and then come back, but I stopped myself.

"Well I hope we can be friends," he said. The tiger kitten was meowing in his box, and he turned to put it in the back of his car. Then he turned toward me again, becoming taller, larger, more apparent. I stood still. There was a feeling of romance in the air—a kind of instant Hollywood romance I hadn't felt since I was a teenager. I was sure he was going to kiss me and I was sure I wouldn't resist.

But all he said was: "Will you please come to visit? Will you bring your little boy? Say yes."

The house seemed quiet when I came upstairs. We had only one kitten left, the elegant one, and he sat by the fireplace looking lonely. I picked him up and brought him to Seth's bedroom and told Seth that now this kitten was his and he was going to have to take care of it.

"Why do cats move their tails?" Seth asked, sitting up in bed. "Do they have bones in them? Or what?"

"I think they have cartilage in them," I said. "And I think they move their tails to get their balance."

Seth paused for a moment, sensing I wasn't sure. Then he asked: "Hey, mommy—how come Ms. Pacman keeps coming back? How come she doesn't disappear after she's eaten up?"

"Because Ms. Pacman is eternal, honey: She's made of light."

"That's what I thought," said Seth, hooking his elbow through mine and jerking me down so I was lying next to him. He held me so tightly, and his elbow was so small, I had the sense of being pinioned by an angel. I almost fell asleep, lying next to him, and when the phone rang and it was Walker, I was able to tell him where he was.

"How did you know?" he asked.

"I've learned to guess," I answered.

ABERRATIONS OF LIGHT

SHE HAD NO IDEA WHAT PROMPTED HER TO ASK—AFTER all these months—why he slept with the light on. All this time, never sleeping in the dark, and she hadn't mentioned it at all. He was undressing carefully, the way he always did, and she looked up from her wildlife magazine, watching him jerk at a cufflink. "Charles! Why do you sleep with the light on?"

He stood poised looking at her, then pulled off the cufflink, tossed it in an earthenware pot. "Why? Why do you ask?"

She hesitated, looked at him over the magazine. "I just realized I've never been with you once without seeing you except when we talk on the phone. I guess I think that's strange."

"Some people don't like the dark."

"Why? Does it make you nervous?"

"No. Not exactly."

"Scared then?"

"No. Not that either." He was taking off his dark green shirt, and he paused with one hand half-way in the sleeve. For a moment he seemed sad. "Okay, you might as well know," he said. Then he turned off the light.

Ruth caught her breath. In the dark, his skin emanated a phosphorescent glow—green and silvery like marsh light. His blond hair and moustache were filaments, a pool of light surrounded him on the floor. His pubic hairs were incandescent.

"My God! I never knew," she said.

He shrugged and stood before her calmly, as if he accepted his condition, even welcomed it. It was clear that his secrecy had nothing to do with embarrassment. She touched him and his skin was cool. "I never knew," she said again.

"Really? I thought maybe you already did." And then—as though revelation made the whole thing seem unremarkable—he sat on the bed and stretched his arms, spreading light into the room. She could see her own arms in the reflection. They didn't look like her arms and she pulled them away.

"You thought I knew! You thought I'd notice something like that and never mention it?"

"I don't know. You've done that with other things."

"Like what? What other things?"

"I don't know. You would be the one to know." He brooded for a moment, then patted her. "Of course I knew you didn't know—it was just that I wanted you to."

"That's okay." She pressed her fingers against his palms and felt a flood of love.

Ruth worked as a naturalist for a wildlife association in the city. She took octagenarians bird-watching and children on hikes by the beach. Now she groped for analogies from the natural world—luminous insects, electric eels, iridescent fish. Marsh light is the best way to think about this, she decided—or maybe something external, something from the atmosphere.

"Have you seen a doctor about this?"

"Why?"

"Because I just wondered. Did you?"

"As a matter of fact I did, but he didn't believe me. I mean this thing comes and goes—and it wasn't happening at the time. We even pulled down the shades, and went into the guy's closet. But nothing happened and he thought I was nuts."

Ruth had a vivid image of Charles and the doctor in a closet which contained medical charts, the doctor's skis, and several coats. She wondered if the doctor was Mark Ehrenfeld, their friend, who'd given them blood tests when they'd been thinking of getting married. She asked if it was and he said it wasn't.

"Are you crazy? I'd never go to someone I knew. It was a cousin of this woman I knew from law school."

"Did you tell *her*?"

"Jesus. You think I go around talking about this? Of course not."

He turned away from her and lay against the pillows, casting light on her arms, the bedside table, and the sheets she'd bought before she'd moved in with him. The sheets were a floral pattern and she'd hesitated before buying them—she was afraid they would seem too romantic and Charles would object. But he had said nothing, and now light from his body seemed to be giving the sheets his tacit approval.

"Charles. Do you like these sheets?"

"How come?"

"Oh, I just wondered," she answered, unable to explain that mentioning one unspeakable subject made it possible to mention another. She'd spent almost an hour thinking about the sheets, wandering over to the shower curtains, then going back. Finally she'd thrust her charge-card at the salesperson and said, "Look. I want those sheets, the ones with the flowers."

Now Charles raised his legs so the sheets became a tent, then disappeared inside. She looked in too, touched a pubic hair. He jumped.

"What's the matter?"

"Nothing."

"Well can't I show some affection?" He didn't answer and she went on. "For God's sakes, I've been patient all these months, never bugging you, sleeping with the damned light on. Can't I touch you when you're all lit up?"

"No. At least not right now." He pulled away, wrapped himself in the sheets. She crept closer and he grudgingly let her massage his back. His back felt normal, just like any other human back.

"You're fine," she said.

"What do you mean?"

"I mean I can feel your muscles."

He shrugged, still brooding, and she remembered a blue electric eel she'd seen off the coast of Cosa Mel last year. Charles reminded her of that eel, but not in a way she liked.

"Hey, listen, do you still love me?" she asked.

"What?"

I said: "Do you love me?"

He sat up. Furrows of light appeared on his brow. "For God's sake, Ruth, give me a break. I'm letting you *in* on something. Don't grill me."

"I'm sorry. Really. I am." She tried to hug him, but he pulled away and began to touch his face. First his mouth, then his eyes, then his mouth. The process was tentative, slow, experimental. She distracted herself by lighting one of his cigarettes and concentrating on the glow: If she looked at him through the end of the cigarette, he was less lit-up, almost normal-looking.

"Won't you talk?"

"No, I won't." He stopped touching his face, reached for the cigarette. They smoked in silence until suddenly he went dark, leaving them both in primal blackness.

"My God!"

"I told you. It comes and goes."

"How long does it last?" she tried to make her voice sound casual.

He shrugged—a gesture which she couldn't see, but could intuit—and then, as if the darkness bothered him too, he turned on the light and picked up her magazine on wildlife. He leafed through an article on pandas, found something about an African lemur. He began to read in earnest. She watched his mouth relax.

"Is this how things are going to wind up tonight?"

"What do you mean?"

"I mean never mind. I'm going for a walk."

"Now? It's late."

"That's the point."

She went to their walk-in closet for a pair of jeans and happened to notice the clothes he'd been wearing hanging from a hook. They were emanating silver light, the shirt buttons glowed like moons. "Your clothes!" she cried. "They're all lit up."

"I know," he said, sounding sad and far-away. "They stay lit longer than I do. . . . Listen, Ruth, don't go out. Look, there's something I want to tell you."

"What?"

"Something personal. I can't tell you unless you come out here."

Ruth stayed in the closet, looking at Charles's clothes, then knelt down and put them on. Their light surrounded her, made her feel buoyant, translucent.

She shimmered past Charles to the porch and looked at the sky—black, without a single star. She was thinking maybe she would walk to the reservoir, surprise lovers, startle vagrants, when Charles came outside and began to kiss her—slowly, methodically, with deep, unprecedented passion. His body was dark, a darkness she could almost taste, and she found it eerie, wild and strange to touch him without seeing him. It was like reading braille, she thought, learning his skin like a language; and when he made her promise to wear his clothes again and again, tomorrow night, and the night after that, she told him yes, of course she would.

A BRIEF HISTORY
OF CAMOUFLAGE

SHE DIDN'T REMEMBER WHEN SHE DECIDED TO MAKE A a dress that matched the colors of her favorite living room chair. Maybe one night, when she was sitting in it reading, watching her husband from the other end of the room. Or maybe on a different night, when she was sitting opposite that chair, looking at it. The chair was covered in muted greens and golds, not the purples and blues she usually wore. She sat there looking at it and decided she would look nice in a dress with the same colors.

The next day she left work early and went to a dry-goods store. She almost never sewed and it felt strange to enter a world where women murmured over patterns and fingered fabrics. She spent a long time choosing material and finally bought some green and gold semitransparent silk. She also bought a pattern for a chair from an upholstery book. The next night she wore what she had made and sat in the chair that matched its colors. Her husband stared in her direction for a long time. Finally he said: You blend with those colors almost perfectly. She smiled and said she knew that.

She enjoyed resembling the chair, but at some point she discovered a stronger force inside her—a force that wanted to look exactly like it: She added sleeves that looked like the arm rests, and made a green and gold hat with matching veil. That night she sat in the chair watching her husband stare into space and he didn't notice her at all. Clearly he thought he was alone, and at some point she felt guilty for spying and cried out: Where am I? He jumped up and looked around the room, but he couldn't find her. Where are you? he kept asking. Over here, she answered. Finally she got up and he thought the chair was walking: He only believed it was her when she took off the veil. She felt vaguely guilty about what she'd done, but she was curious about what he was like when he was alone. So she began to wear the matching outfit and sit in the chair without telling him. She discovered that his private face was sad and his eyes seemed more transparent. Usually he read, but sometimes he spoke out loud, saying things like: What? or: I didn't want to do that. Once he delivered an angry monologue about a bar of soap she'd allowed to disintegrate in the sink. I can't live this way, he said. You never do what I ask. She decided she would try to be more careful.

She enjoyed being the chair, but she wanted to be other things too: She made a dress that matched the living room blinds, with cords and slats that could be opened and shut, and a jumpsuit that looked like their couch, with bolsters on the shoulders. These clothes were uncomfortable, but comfort wasn't the point: They allowed her to get to know her husband. Over time, he got used to seeing less of her and talked out loud more often. Mostly he talked about things that annoyed him, but one night he had an imaginary conversation with a woman who lived down the street: I really can't come over, he said, because I'm married. Then, imitating the woman's voice, he answered: But I know how you really feel about me. I've seen you watch my legs when I get into my car.

She listened quietly, disguised as any number of things. He talked about his favorite movies and his track records in college and arguments at his office. He talked about a pie-eating contest he'd won in high school and a Maserati he intended to buy. One night while she was sitting on the couch wearing the outfit with the bolsters, he said: I have to think things over, so I'm going to go to the mountains. That's right, I really have to think. He said this a couple of times, then went to the attic and got a duffel bag. She rushed to the bedroom, put on a robe that matched their curtains and stood by the window. Soon he came in with the suitcase, pulled clothes out of their closet and began to pack. He packed a lot of familiar clothes, mostly sweaters and jeans, but he also packed some clothes she'd never seen and didn't seem like anything he'd wear in the mountains: a striped vintage suit that looked like it had belonged to a gangster, and the kind of sweater-vest he always said he'd never be caught dead in. He stuffed the familiar clothes carelessly in the duffel bag, but packed the new things carefully as though they might be fragile. He also packed books and shaving cream and toothpaste, and a carton of after-dinner mints, which she'd never known him to eat. The whole procedure took over half an hour.

She watched without a word. When he was through, he zipped up the duffel bag and said: Well, that does it. I'm going to go to the mountains now. He left the house and she heard his car revving up in the driveway. As soon as it drove away, sounding like a dangerous muzzled beast, she took off the curtains, drank some wine, then put on the outfit that matched the chair. Perhaps because he wasn't there she didn't feel like herself at all—she simply blended with the chair, and knew what it felt like to be it. The same was true of all her other disguises, and she found this restful.

During the day, she had to go to work and run errands, but as soon as she came home, she put on whatever she wanted to become and sat down with a glass of wine. Over time she began to experience the house as though she were inanimate: She got to know its changing gradients of light, and special sounds, especially at night, when it seemed to sigh and shift on its foundation. From this vantage point, she sometimes stared out the window and saw the woman her husband liked walking down the street. She felt a sense of pity for her, pity mixed with dispassion.

One day her husband called and said he wanted to come back. He had thought things over and he really missed her. She told him she'd prefer that he didn't, because she'd entered another realm. He asked what she meant, and she answered: *The realm of the inanimate.* He persisted, saying that life wasn't the same without her, and finally she told him that of course he could come home, but he would hardly ever see her. He said that was okay, certainly better than nothing.

He called on a Tuesday and came back over the weekend. She was waiting for him in the chair, wearing the fabric that matched it: and as soon as he opened the door he walked over to the chair, kissed her and said that she couldn't fool him, he could see her. She looked into his eyes, and knew, from the reflection in his pupils, he wasn't seeing her, but was seeing the entire house, crystalline in detail, glittering, complete. Under the circumstances it was fine to kiss him, too, and she did, again and again, loving as only inanimate objects can love—mutely, impartially, without wanting anything back.

A FABLE

IN A SENSE IT WAS A MARRIAGE MADE IN HEAVEN: HE
wanted to be loved but not known, and she wanted to
be known but not loved. Neither of them knew this
when they first got married, they both thought they
wanted the same thing—but one night, after two years
of violent fighting, they had a truth-telling session and
the whole thing came out. The worst part was that they
realized that their love-making had been a sham:
Subliminally, through invisible membranes, they were
always trying to correct the mistakes they'd made during the day.

After having this talk they decided to visit
the same hotel where they'd spent their honeymoon. They drove up the coast and saw the same
beautiful spring fields and the same perfectly-
arranged cows and, at last, the same hotel where
screeching peacocks roamed the grounds. They got a
different room, walked around the garden, talked
about how they could change things. She felt hope-
less, but he suggested that they make a pact: She
would agree not to try to love him and he would agree

not to try to know her—they would do whatever they wanted.

They did well during dinner, better over wine. But when they got into bed, she had a profound experience of his reluctance to be known, and he had the same overwhelming sense of her reluctance to be loved. This made them uncomfortable, and they began to talk about other lovers—women who had loved him, men who had known her. Talking made them excited and when they embraced they felt all these other men and women, tangled in their arms. Love and knowledge felt the same. Where do we go from here? she asked. Wherever we want to, he answered.

II.
NIGHT VISITS

. . . out of rock
Out of a desolate source,
Love leaps upon its course

—*Yeats*

AN AFTERNOON IN KANSAS

WHEN I WAS THREE YEARS OLD, A FEW YEARS AFTER THE end of the Second World War, and old enough to understand, my mother tried to strangle me. It was late afternoon, the raw nerves, hard for her in the middle of Kansas. I was in my crib, crying. She came in the room, looked over me. Then, from the ceiling of my bedroom, I saw my own half-crazed eyes as her hand twisted my head, pressed her thumb against my throat, pushed my chin into my neck. My doll caved against my ribs, an ally of sorts, with hard, plastic fingers.

This was a time of intense silence: Bits of air, meant for me, fanned around my mother's throat. Her eyes, framed in slanted glasses, were dark, electric, furious. Maybe I made a deep appeal, asking her to let me live. Or maybe we met in some mysterious, ineffable harmony. In any case, the phone rang, and her hands loosened.

Later my father walked me around the living room. He wanted to see if I could move my neck. I could.

Afterwards, I only remembered I'd swallowed a bubble of air that kept me from breathing. I felt it when I was at the movies, or on long walks through Kansas fields—or in a flash, when I saw dead animals. Years later, I looked in the mirror, saw my mother's face above my own, remembered the deep vitality of her eyes in that moment above my crib. For an instant her face became my face, her eyes became my eyes. And then she separated out, became miraculously herself. Never again have I seen another person more clearly.

MY FACE

WINTERS WERE BLEAK IN THE MIDWEST. THERE WERE days when the furniture lost its edges early, and everything got dark by four. Then, until the lamps did their work, everything was obscure, and my mother often sat in the living room staring into space. She didn't like winter because it was confining.

"What is confining?" I asked.

"Too small. The kind of small that makes you nervous."

I was small. And I knew that I made her nervous. Therefore I deduced that I, too, was confining, and tried to make myself scarce. I sat on the other side of the dark room watching her, wondering what else was going on behind her vacant, darting eyes. It seemed that she looked ahead to places she would never reach, back to places she had never been. I could imagine a world in front of her eyes, but I didn't want to enter it. Like the day, it was dark and barren.

Outside, the old French peasant who kept chickens in the heart of suburban Kansas came out to gather her five o'clock eggs. I could see her kerchiefed head bobbing up and down, while her chickens flocked around her. I was never sure whether she actually gathered eggs, or performed some act of obeisance as she bent toward the ground. With something, or perhaps nothing, in her basket, she hobbled back to the house. My mother looked out the window and sighed.

Meanwhile men returning from work began to walk down the avenue opposite the alley. It was a promenade, a promenade of hats and newspapers— and I watched them, hoping to see my father. But my mother didn't notice: Her gaze went somewhere beyond the window—to an opera house, where women in tiered gowns fanned themselves, or to a London street where Pears' soap was displayed in shop windows. Her century wasn't this one: She bought cheap earrings that duplicated the patterns of chandeliers. She liked glass that looked like crystal.

Sometimes my mother slipped into evening without a trace. Then she was gathered up by the walls and couldn't be distinguished from the faded green brocade of the couch. Her near-disappearance was accompanied by listlessness and a sense of abstract grief. Her eyes, which in fact were small, grew large, and I was never sure whether this was a theatrical expression or sadness. As for my father, when he came home to find her in these states, he always seemed bewildered. As though her revival were imminent, he padded around the kitchen opening cans of soup, ferreting out boxes of stale crackers.

"Would you like some soup, Marlie dear?"

"No."

"A little bouillon?"

"Maybe later."

My father's voice was tense and cheerful—an affront to the tragedies my mother witnessed. Had there been a fireplace, he and I would have sat in front of it looking at the flames, further denying her grief. But instead we sat in the small kitchen, painfully aware of her presence on the couch.

I often thought that the present night, in which the moon rose over the chicken coop and my father and I ate our soup, was only a convenience—something to create the illusion that my mother actually existed. In truth, the real night was somewhere else, and my mother—on the couch under the wedding scene by Breughel—was an imperious ward of that night with special privileges. Once I saw her staring at the chicken coop across the alley, and as she stared the pattern of moonlight changed directions on the rug. I wondered if her voice continued to speak inside her head, invoking the night, asking it to protect her.

At other times the approach of evening didn't quiet my mother at all. The furniture refused to absorb her, and the walls didn't let her fade. As if the night wanted to expel her, her hawk nose became sharper, her eyes became brighter, and her thick hands became unbearably distinct. Having lost control over the night, she turned her attention to her surroundings. She

called our apartment a slum, and denounced my father
—who was absent—for not finding us a better house.

Once, after a frightening oral inventory of
everything in the room, during which the furniture
seemed to stiffen and even the ashtrays looked polite,
she wrung her hands and looked at the ceiling as if
invoking a family of bats. In the hall neighbors
paused—discreetly, for the boards creaked.

I wanted a place to hide. Soon my mother's voice
would blow in my direction, like a monsoon. In spite
of her cluttered closets, her memory was neat. Nothing
I had ever done, or not done, eluded her:

"I begged you to leave the house, but you insisted
on trying on those gloves. Those crummy dime-store
gloves. Pieces of cheap felt! I begged you and begged
you and begged you but you tried them on. *Hours* while
I waited in the hall. Hours! We missed the bus! We
missed the bus! You tried on those gloves and we
missed the bus!"

I stood still as the small maple chest in the hall.
Last week, in the heat of her tirade, she decided I
wasn't clean. She flew at me, undressed me, invading
me with soap and language. But such scenes were
reserved for the greatest of miseries, the nameless,
wrenching kind that could only be relieved by an
assault on other body. Today she turned her attention
to the smaller objects, all of whom witnessed her like
frightened rabbits.

"Look at this!" she said, picking up a clock and

throwing it against the wall. "Everything cluttered in this tiny room! Everything in a heap!"

The clock fell to the floor—still, aparently itself, only now with a hairline of glass across its face. Obediently, it kept on ticking.

"Books!" she said. "Books and magazines everywhere!" The books were in the bookcase, their embossed titles looking at her like eyes. She glared at them, picked up a magazine and rattled it: "This thing! This goddam thing!" she repeated, holding it in front of her and shaking the pages as though the book were a head of hair.

———

Usually I found myself in the same position as the objects: motionless, mute enduring with a sense of apology. But on this particular afternoon, as I watched my mother hover between absorption and exile, I went calmly to her room and sat in front of her dressing table. All of her make-up was laid out in front of me— her mascaras, her eye-liners, her powder. Also a small cut-glass pot of rouge—a rouge so red, so dark, so fragrant, it promised unholy forms of transformation. Without ceremony I opened it and began to rub it on my face. The effect was fascinating. Like an etching becoming visible, I saw myself all radiant and red and strange, flying under the flag of another country.

The night had refused to absorb my mother. When I came back to the living room, she'd just assaulted one of her black, high-heeled shoes (those shoes that embarrassed me whenever I saw them), and was about to attack another one.

"This life!" she cried. "How I loathe and despise this life!"

She didn't see me, and I stood as still as the shoe waiting to be thrown. Red radiated from my face to my feet, riveting me to the ground. As my mother turned to pick up the shoe, she saw me.

"Get that red off your face!" she cried. "Go inside and wash that red off!"

I didn't move. Inhabited by a power I didn't understand, I stayed still, compressed, hard as stone. I felt small, yet billions of years old, like an alien and stubborn star. My mother stood poised, holding the shoe. I stood in front of her, radiating.

Suddenly my mother started to laugh. It was an amazing laugh, as though her skin were about to crack open and lay bare her bones, as though something deep inside of her had burst. I stared at her, and she laughed and laughed and laughed, as though night were pouring out of her, from her bones to mine.

ORIGINS

WHEN I WAS A CHILD, I THOUGHT OUR FAMILY HAD NO origins. Not in the sense that we had no ancestors, but in the sense that nothing of the past assured the present. Other families, it seemed, had something behind them, something that said to them: "This is us!" But for my family the sun rose every morning as if by accident. Days began from scratch. Living was imbued with a perilous sense of adventure.

On mornings when my mother happened to get up, she always surveyed the house as though it were an enormous jigsaw puzzle—the kind that took months, even years, to complete. Rummaging through my dresser drawers, she would despair of finding what I needed for my day at school. "Your shoes!" she would cry. "Your socks! This room is like a bird's nest."

And indeed the whole house felt like a nest. Not a cozy, down-filled robin's nest, but the nest of a chaotic bird. Yet the cry of *nest!* had curious powers: Clothes would be found, a pair of matching socks would be produced. And borne by the grace of these rituals, I would be out the door walking to school.

Miraculously, my shoes enclosed my feet, my clothes surrounded my body. By the time I got to school, any memory of my mother and the house (now cool and dark, my mother back in bed) was a dream, a half-life.

On mornings when my mother didn't get up I had to invoke the day alone. While she slept (and it was a deep, amazing sleep, that elongated the ceilings and stretched the walls) I opened the drawers and weeded my way through a maze of clothes. Bit by bit, as though it were forbidden, I invented myself from whatever I happened to find. I never invoked the terrible cry of *nest!* but used an incantation of my own, whispering about what I was doing.

═══════

Breakfast was never possible in the process of reconstruction. If my mother happened to be up, eating was an affront to her notion of what people were supposed to be doing at that hour, and if I was alone, it was too real and too lonely to attempt. The only times I ever encountered breakfast were the rare mornings when my father was home. His offerings consisted of real food; but the breakfasts struck me as being only memories of breakfasts from his own childhood which I knew (by some osmotic sense) had approached normalcy. My father would set out grapefruit, orange juice, and cornflakes (the latter he called "breakfast food"), start to eat, and urge me to do the same. But I couldn't because the food struck me as being simply representational—that is, as *standing* for food, rather than *being* it.

"Eat," my father would urge, appealing to his origins.

"Daddy, I'm not hungry, I can't."

========

My father and I sat in the kitchen with a sense of apologetic conspiracy: Tucked away in the northeast corner of the house, my mother slept in a darkened room. This room had the feeling of a chapel and there was the sense that something more important than sleep was going on there. It was both glorious and terrifying, the way my mother transcended ordinary notions of time and space, and wrested her portion of the night, from the night, and hauled it back into the day. Often when I was at school—singing songs, doing arithmetic, copying impossible sketches of animals— I'd think of her at home in bed. I worried that she would become confused, wake up, and appear in class in her see-through rose-colored nightgown. This image of her blooming in the classroom like a strange transparent rose persisted for many years.

My friend, Kathy Montague, had origins. I knew this not just from the pictures in her hall: brown and yellowing ancestors, women from Ohio with mouths like mail slots. It was something else, something in the air around her. Her mother's name was Margaret. She made melted-cheese sandwiches with strips of cut-up bacon on them, cooked pancakes with fluted edges, and bought Kathy ruffled dresses which she ironed, carefully, diligently, while Kathy and I played.

"Why do you want to be like *her*?" my mother asked, catching on to my desires, when I asked for a dress with ruffles. "Kathy Montague is a very dull, precise little girl. She counts when she does ballet and she always colors inside the lines."

I decided that I, too, would be dull and precise. I began to count when I did ballet and I got a coloring book and colored inside the lines. I made everything red, even the trees.

My life as Kathy Montague was only the beginning of a long career in which I assumed strange names and wore impossible disguises. But my mother remained the master of reversals: she could perform the same sleight-of-hand trick with the night, as she did with the day, and when everyone else in Kansas had gone to bed and the sun was assaulting the Indian

Ocean, she came to life. From my little bedroom (an alcove with a blanket tacked over it to shield the light) I could hear her only three feet away. She read Dickens, Austen, Thackeray, Agatha Christie. She cracked walnuts and disappeared into the kitchen. There was rustling, crunching, coughing and sometimes she would laugh.

"Mother, what are you eating now?" I would cry.

"Walnuts. Now go to sleep."

But I couldn't sleep. It seemed incumbent to stay up with her while she celebrated her life. I lay in bed, surrounded by all my animals, listening to her, being with her, imagining what she was doing. At midnight a certain Tchaikovsky waltz came on the radio and I could feel her winding down. The pages turned more slowly. The chewing stopped.

One night my mother came into my room, sat on my bed and looked at me. My stuffed animals left almost no room for her. She sat way on the edge of the bed.

"Why don't you sleep at night?" she asked. "What's wrong with you?"

The Tchaikovsky waltz came on. Lovely, delicate, from an earlier time. All I could give my mother were my eyes. We looked at each other for a while, and then she said: "You're tired in the morning."

"You are, too," I answered.

"Oh, well . . . *that*," said my mother, as though her tiredness were to be expected. "But I can sleep. You have to go to school."

I nodded. She stood up, and stayed poised in the arched alcove looking at me. Then she went back to the living room. Suddenly I called out:

"But I want to be with you!"

There was a pause, a turned page, an intake of breath. And then my mother's voice, softer, less far away.

"Children need their sleep. But grown-ups can do what they want to."

"But I wish you would make me sandwiches!"

"*Sandwiches*?" said my mother. "You want me to make you sandwiches?"

"Yes. I want you to make me sandwiches."

My mother went to the kitchen and made a radish sandwich with rye bread and cream cheese. She brought it to my bed with a glass of milk.

"I shouldn't be doing this," she said, setting it by my bed.

"Why not?" I said. "It's just like breakfast."

"Yes. . . . I suppose it is."

One morning, a few weeks later, I heard noises in the kitchen, and found my mother making me breakfast. It wasn't my father's sort of breakfast. It was hard rolls with jam, butter and cheese—like the European breakfasts that her mother had given her. She sat in front of me fully dressed, drinking coffee.

"What happened?" I asked.

"Nothing," she said, sounding vaguely insulted.

That morning when I went to school, I had origins. Not the shadowy origins of our ancestors— strange Jews with beards on my mother's side, rigid Presbyterians on my father's side—but tangible roots in a house not far away. My mother was up doing chores. She was ironing, cleaning, mending, baking. She would shop and greet other mothers at the store, maybe even learn to drive a car. I envisioned the beginning of a very different life and was surprised when I came home to find her asleep. It was noon, and she had taken a piece of the night back to bed with her. I stood there, watching her sleep, absorbed in a covenant she couldn't break, while the rest of us were trapped in daylight.

THE KISS

WHEN I WAS SIX I KISSED, WITHOUT WARNING, A BOY named Jerry in the hall of our apartment building. The night before I had seen a naked, half-paralyzed man being bathed by his elderly mother in a wide-open window while hiding in the bushes with my friend. The next day, I found Jerry in the hall and kissed him.

Jerry was nine years old. His breath smelled of mint gum and he had slanted, lizard eyes. He wore a leather jacket and claimed he came from Baghdad, which I knew to exist from *The Arabian Nights*. When I kissed him I thought I could feel a rim of extra teeth inside his mouth, although I never looked too closely: the extra teeth suggested a second person, hidden deep inside him.

"What's your phone number?" he asked as soon as I'd kissed him.

"I don't know."

"Go upstairs and ask your mom."

"Why do you want to know?" my mother asked when I went upstairs. She was leafing through a copy of the *Ladies' Home Journal,* and looking mildly depressed.

"I need it for a library card."

She told me our phone number and I ran downstairs, panted the number to Jerry. He said he'd call and never did.

As soon as I came upstairs my mother seemed to be living in another country—a stark barren country I couldn't name, altering our house, particularly our kitchen. The walls were dingy, the lights were dim. There were old lace curtains in the kitchen, a hunk of black bread on the table. From the window, even though it was summer, I saw children who had no toys—war orphans, I thought—inventing games in the snow. I was sure my mother saw them, too, for she pulled the venetian blinds high. That afternoon I sat in the living room staring at Breughel's wedding picture, which stayed the same; but whenever I looked at the rest of the house, this other country reappeared. For a year it came and went like something in a flip-book. Anything could bring it on. The faintest glimmer of a lie. A tone of voice with an edge to it.

In second grade I knew an underling named Karen, a child who was thin, small, had dark plaited hair and a hesitant way of speaking. She could easily have been a war orphan, but she lived in America, like us. One day, while two of my friends hit Karen with her own umbrella, I watched, not trying to stop them. She ran off, crying in the snow.

I looked at her in her bright green jacket, running away in the dazzling snow, certain she was going to that other country; but it was to this country that her mother wrote a note to the teacher, naming everyone who had been involved, including me. My friends, who were more cunning, lied and said I had hit Karen with the umbrella. The teacher believed them, I was powerless to say no, and I came home and told my mother the truth. She wrote the teacher a note which I delivered, too frightened to read. I never knew if the note released me from my friends' lie or bound me to it.

After this incident the other country receded. Perhaps I had been redeemed, one lie exchanged for another. Or perhaps I had entered a third country where lies were as commonplace as Kansas. In any case, our kitchen became our kitchen again: an ordinary midwestern kitchen, with white pre-sliced bread, linoleum on the floor, venetian blinds at the windows. Our windows looked out to a flat midwestern street. No war orphans played in the snow. But later, when I began to meet men and more lies came between me and my mother, I re-entered that unnamed country—and I still can go there. In that country my mother sits by a window looking at a landscape she's never seen. She sews for me, cooks for me, gives credence to my lies. Her bread is bitter and always dark.

THE ENCHANTED MAN

AT THE END OF THE BLOCK OF MY CHILDHOOD, LIKE A ship forever sailing towards the avenue, was the stately Victorian house of the antique dealer, Adrienne Glass. She didn't use this house for her antique store—that was at the other end of town. But she did use it for storing four-poster beds from every corner of the world. Through the bay window of her living room I often saw such a bed, covered with brocade, near a stand with a vase of flowers that matched the color of the spread. These flowers were made of glass, like Adrienne's last name.

I was six years old, too little to speculate whether the beds had any visitors. But one day, Danny Johnson, who was twelve, made up a song that everybody sang:

> *Old lady Glass has five hundred beds*
> *Eighty for her fingers*
> *Eighty for her head*
> *Eighty for her toes*
> *Eighty for her feet*

And the rest for her bum
When she walks it down the street

This song wasn't right on a couple of counts. First Adrienne Glass wasn't old, she was young; and second she was lean and beautiful and self-sufficient and needed no help transporting any part of her person anywhere. Half the year she spent in Europe shopping for antiques, and once, according to my mother, she'd gotten involved with a German art dealer, just so she could buy his bed, and when the roads outside his villa were snowed-in, she'd hired three students from Heidelberg to portage the bed through a forest.

Mostly, Adrienne Glass kept to herself. But from time to time she visited another house on our block—a house that was notable in suburban Kansas because its backyard was used for keeping live chickens. The few times she visited she always came out with something old: once an enormous oak umbrella stand, once a large gilt mirror which reflected—briefly—the flat midwestern sky. After she left, the owner of the house, a Mrs. D'Agnelli, stood in the doorway, looking after her. She came from Bordeaux, and addressed her chickens every morning in a stream of French. My mother explained that Adrienne Glass was buying Mrs. D'Agnelli's antiques, and she said this with a darkness that we children seized upon. For Mrs. D'Agnelli was an object of interest quite apart from her chickens: She was said to keep a man who was enchanted. This man was young. His name was Armand. And all day long he sat in a silver chair with wheels the size of spinning wheels. My mother said this chair was a wheelchair, and if Mrs. D'Agnelli would only get a chair-lift, Armand could mingle in the neighborhood. "But the French are very *closed*," she said, "and that's the problem."

It was my girlfriend, Christine Haag, who got the notion that Armand was enchanted. And this was because a nun at her school gave a talk about entering the age of reason. Christine, who was eight, had entered that age a year ago, and I, at six, had a year to wait. This nun had said that when one entered the age of reason a kind of grace was bestowed, a grace that allowed you to know what you really wanted; but that sometimes people lost this grace and then they floated around like someone who was enchanted. This information impressed Christine, and she soon applied it to Armand.

"Armand can't think," she said to me one day, "he does everything Mrs. D'Agnelli says. She gives him pears, he eats the pears, she gives him glue, he eats the glue. Just you watch, Armand is a zombie."

I had never seen Armand eat glue, but I felt obliged to believe Christine. My status as a non-Catholic frightened me: With the blessing of her priest, Christine gave me a plastic cross that glowed in the dark. I kept the cross under my bed, and at night, when I was sure my mother wouldn't see me, I would crouch on the floor and look at it.

For Christmas that year, I'd been given a little castle which was set up in such a way so you could tell the weather. When it was about to rain, a white-haired woman emerged from the door; and when it was sunny, two dark-haired children appeared. Whenever I thought of Armand and Mrs. D'Agnelli, I thought of this castle—as though each were opposite ends of the weather. Mrs. D'Agnelli had a beautiful face with snow-white hair, and Armand was handsome and dark, like the children. But he also looked like the prince in my picture book who kissed Snow White awake, and this gave me the idea that enchanted people could be two different ages at once, as well as free other people from a spell. Armand was impeccably dressed, as though he were about to leave for work. Christine was sure he was sitting on the porch, waiting for us to free him.

In the dark place beneath Christine's back porch —a place where we showed each other underwear and whispered secrets—Christine told me stories about Armand. She discounted the rumor that Armand was Mrs. D'Agnelli's oldest son and had once been a public accountant, in favor of the idea that Armand was Mrs. D'Agnelli's nephew. He had been rich, she said, and Mrs. D'Agnelli had bewitched him for his money. The story was embellished with Christine's notions of France—old stone castles, people with pointed hats. Christine said that whenever she passed Armand he looked at her, and she knew by his eyes he was waiting for us to free him. "He has a special way of saying things. He talks in a secret code. . . ."

We never went up to talk to Armand. He seemed happy on the porch, by himself, dreaming his private dream, and it was enough to know that Christine and I shared a secret. Of course, in addition to this secret, I had a secret of my own, which was that I sometimes thought of going to live with Armand after I had saved him.

It was Adrienne Glass who provided us with absolute evidence that Armand was enchanted. One winter afternoon she drove to the D'Agnelli's house in her black antique-store truck with gold letters on the side, and came out with an amazing-looking chair which she carried downstairs by herself. After shoving the chair into the truck, she removed a large porcelain pitcher, went back up the stairs, and handed it to Mrs. D'Agnelli. My mother said that the chair ws a valuable 19th-century privy chair, and the pitcher was a gift because Adrienne Glass felt sorry that Mrs. D'Agnelli had to sell her last heirloom—for Armand, she said, who needed oxygen.

It was clear to Christine that one instrument of enchantment had merely been exchanged for another: "People always make their spells in special chairs," she said, "and later they use some water, a little like holy water, except the priest would never bless it." We were sitting beneath her porch, shelling peas and eating most of them. I looked at Christine and thought that she looked like the saint above her bed. Curly blond hair, a few freckles, blue eyes that gave the impression of informed intelligence.

"My mother says the chair was for a chamber pot," I said. "People used to use it for going to the bathroom."

"That's because the bathroom is where they do their spells," said Christine. She dropped a pea-pod on the ground and looked at me. "Never let anyone come to the bathroom with you," she said, "even when you're sick. Just pray and pray to God that you're not going to vomip."

Ever since I'd known her, Christine had pronounced vomit "vomip." But I was at a loss to correct her, because somehow, when pronounced that way, the word became unspeakable.

One day, in late spring, something made me decide to visit Armand by myself. He was sitting on the porch, and I stood below the stairs until he noticed me. Then he nodded his head—rigidly, the way a bird will nod. And I took this as an invitation to come up.

The stairs to the D'Agnelli's house were steep, with spaces between them like a ladder. As I walked up, I was afraid I might fall through one of the holes. When I got to the top I discovered how small the porch was—about the size of the stair-lift that would have let Armand mingle in the neighborhood. I also saw that his view of the block was the same view I had from my bedroom window.

"Hello there," said Armand.

"Hello," I answered.

Indeed Armand was handsome. But up close his face looked less like the face of a prince and more like the face of a handyman who sometimes came to help my mother. He was wearing a clean white shirt and a brown sweater-vest, and the brown of the vest was the same color as his hair. From where I stood I could see tiny flecks of dandruff—waxy, white, arranged upon the vest like snow. I thought I shouldn't see this, so I turned to face him more directly.

"Do you come here often?" said Armand, pronouncing "often" with a *t*.

"Yes," I said, "I live across the alley."

"That's nice," said Armand. And in that moment I realized that for all we talked about him, he never noticed us.

I turned my head again so I could take another look at Armand's view—the same view I had when I looked out my bedroom window. There was the large white house facing the avenue, the houses facing that house, and beyond those houses the lake. It was the first time I'd realized that someone else could see my world.

"Do you go to school?" Armand asked.

"Yes," I said.

"Where?" he asked.

"At Noyes Street, near the bakery." As soon as I said this, I felt chagrined because Armand had never been to the bakery and didn't know where Noyes Street was. So I pointed in the direction of Noyes Street and Armand looked. It was impossible to see Noyes Street—we could only see the underpass to the railroad. I told him it was beyond the tracks, and described the route.

Suddenly Mrs. D'Agnelli opened the door without a sound, startling me with the whiteness of her hair. She nodded to me, almost bowing, and wheeled Armand into the house. After the door was closed I stood quite still, until suddenly I remembered two things: first that Armand was supposed to be talking in secret code, and second that Mrs. D'Agnelli slaughtered old hens. I ran down the stairs, terrified, and met Christine who had been watching me.

"What happened?" she cried.

"Nothing!"

"But she knows. She suspicions you and she knows."

"Suspicions" sounded dreadful—like it was made

of scissors and knives. I decided I would never talk to Armand again.

That was the summer I turned seven, and all the rest of that year, Armand sat on the porch with his dreamy eyes, and twice I forgot my vow and went upstairs to talk to him. We talked about commonplace things—a tree, a truck, a passing bird. Unlike other adults, whenever Armand talked, he seemed to be talking about *just that thing* and for this reason, I was at a loss to decipher a secret code. Our conversations never lasted long, because Mrs. D'Agnelli always wheeled Armand away. Through the open door I could see a sliver of their narrow hall—dark, with a huge porcelain vase filled with lavender.

In late spring, Armand began to appear on the porch less often—he was weak, my mother said, and needed oxygen. Christine and I lost interest in him. Trading cards occupied us—we especially liked pictures of dogs—and we might have forgotten him completely, except for one summer evening when Mrs. D'Agnelli forgot to draw the curtains on her kitchen window. It was a warm, milky dusk, a time when everything was co-mingling and bursting with light; and Christine and I were playing hopscotch across the street. I had just reached the 4 and was about to throw my skate key on the 5 when I looked up and saw Armand lying naked on a table. He was on his back and his legs, which were covered with dark black hair, were drawn up like a baby about to be diapered. Christine and I crept to the hedge outside the D'Agnelli's garden, with a delicious illicit feeling, that didn't prepare us for what we saw: Mrs. D'Agnelli was washing Armand with her hands. She dipped one hand in Adrienne Glass's porcelain pitcher, and the other in a clear glass bowl, filled with water. She alternated hands, smoothing them over his body, washing, rinsing, while Armand lay quietly, looking at a point on the ceiling as though he weren't in the room at all. After Mrs. D'Agnelli was done washing him, she dried him with a towel, paying special attention to his legs as if she meant to dry every hair. And then she gave Armand a toothbrush which he used to brush his teeth. Twice he took water from a cup which he spat into another cup. When he was done, Mrs. D'Agnelli turned off the overhead light.

All this time, Christine and I had been crouched by the hedge. But when the light went off, we came closer to the house by way of the path. In the near-dark we saw Mrs. D'Agnelli wheeling Armand away. The table seemed to float and as I watched him disappear, I knew that Armand wasn't enchanted, only ill, and that his body wasn't being used and never would be used, in a way that I sensed, even at seven, he wanted to use it. While Christine and I stood in the darkness giggling, I experienced a terrible shaken feeling, as if it had been me, not Armand, lying on the table. That night I pushed Christine's cross to a far corner under my bed, and the next day, impelled by a force I didn't understand, I kissed a boy three years older than I in the hall of my apartment building. It was a heady, passionate kiss, and he received it with aplomb and pleasure. Then he asked me for my phone number, which I didn't know. Afterwards I felt relieved, as though the secret of Armand had been crowded out of my mind, and I regaled Christine with stories about the boy. It was the first time I had ever been able to engage Christine, and over time the stories grew more bold. Armand never appeared on the porch again—or if he did, I never saw him—but the boy I'd kissed grew larger and more amazing in my mind, dark, exotic, always smelling of his leather jacket. Christine listened to me enraptured, and it was only later that year, when Armand died, that I was able to remember that night without any sense of betraying him. Then I could talk about it, and dwell on it, and even admit how beautiful I thought Armand was. And after a while my belief in his enchantment returned, and Adrienne Glass's water pitcher was restored, once more, to the realm of mysterious objects.

THE STORE

THERE WAS ONE PLACE WHERE MY MOTHER NEVER
followed me: a store at the end of a black gravel alley
whose air was soft and quiet, like a library. This store,
the only dark refuge in the bright midwestern summer, had a sweet, stale smell that repelled grown-ups,
and everything sensible, like soap, was on a high inac-
cessible shelf. Only the candies were lit faintly in the
glass cases: there were wax bottles filled with green
liquid, dots of colored sugar on strips of paper, small
dark babies, called by a name I'd been told never to
say. There were chocolate cigarettes, glass jars filled
with hearts.

A man named Sabbey owned the store. As he
was, in fact, very shabby, I gave some credulity to his
name. I never talked when I came into his store: I
pointed. Whatever I pointed to, Sabbey reached for
with his long white hands and put in a paper bag. His
eyes were watery, like a fish's, and his face was so long
it didn't stop at his chin but faded into his neck below
his tie. I paid him with my allowance.

"Thank you," he would say, as though he were

swallowing candy. His lips were always moist.

Outside, in the sun, the candies were still il-luminated. But their edges were defined, and so were their sharp sweet tastes. The green liquid exploded in my mouth, and round bits of sugar clung to the white paper like barnacles. Alone, or with Christine Haag, I walked home feeling the grit of asphalt on my sneakers. The asphalt looked like broken coal, and made us walk in a rhythm that matched our chewing.

One day an unthinkable event occurred: My mother went into Sabbey's store. It was late in the day and she needed soap. While I stood in the door, want-ing to hide, she entered it as she would any store—bustling, announcing herself in that dark. "Hello, Mr. Sabbey," she said. "I would like to buy some soap."

"Soap?" said a voice from the back of the store.

"Soap," said my mother.

A curious waiting silence. Sabbey shuffled from the back of the store, got a step ladder, a stick, and reached to an unknown cavern in the precarious dark. From it he retrieved a bar of soap.

"Thank you," he said, swallowing to my mother. "Thank you very much."

While were walking home through the alley, I instructed my mother that no one called Sabbey "Mr."

"His name is *Sabbey*," I said.

"Sabbey?" said my mother. "Why that's very rude. You should always call him Mr. Sabbey. That's his *name*."

That night at dinner I thought about my mother going into Sabbey's store. The whole scene—viewed from a distance—was extremely vivid. I saw her going in to the store, standing in front of the sacred candies. I heard her voice encircling Sabbey like a wreath. This vision bothered me so much I couldn't even tell Christine, but declined to go in with her the next time she asked.

"Why not?" she wanted to know.

"I can't tell," I said.

For a week, I walked past Sabbey's store, looking the other way, sure he saw me from behind his glass case, remembered the mortifying scene with my mother. At no point would I go in, although Christine begged me.

One day my mother reached into her purse and said that she wanted me to go to Sabbey's and buy toilet paper. Toilet paper! How could I possibly buy toilet paper at Sabbey's? She gave me fifty cents and I walked down the alley; but when I got to the store asking for toilet paper was impossible, so I handed him the money and pointed to a whole jar of cinnamon hearts, which were absolutely forbidden. Sabbey handed me the jar—not knowing he was an accomplice—and suddenly became mine again: fish-like, tall, with his watery way of saying things. On the way home, I stopped by Christine's house, gave her the jar of hearts, begged her for toilet paper. She gave me two rolls and looked me in the eye. I confessed that I had stolen. She promised she would pray for me.

MY MOTHER'S VOICE

I DIDN'T TELL YOU TO TAKE OFF THE HAT NEXT TO THE vegetables," my mother said loudly. "I told you to put it in your pocket once we got inside. But did you listen to me? No, you did not. And now you've lost your hat." She peered at me from the rows of vegetables and continued, magnificent and launched. "Kathy Montague listens to *her* mother. Molly Perone listens to *her* mother. Chickie Messick. . . . Christine Haag. . . ."

The list went on. Names of various children were invoked. All these children listened. "But do you listen? No! You do not! You do *not!*" My mother wore long dangling earrings, bright red lipstick, and rouge kept in a crystal pot from her days at drama school—all of which enhanced her enormous nose, which communicated whatever her voice failed to convey. While she talked, her nose sniffed, snorted and bobbed, and her small eyes blinked rapidly, as if overwhelmed by the nose, possibly propelled by it.

From the other side of the vegetable bin appeared the thin, unhappy face of Mr. Hummerford. Mr. Hummerford was from England and had impeccable manners, which meant, in this case, that he regarded us as space aliens.

"Is this the hat?" he asked, pulling a blue beret with a crest of ice from some broccoli.

"Why yes," my mother said. "It is."

"I think it fell out of your coat," he said.

He meant my mother's coat. She put the hat in her shopping bag as though it were an onion.

═══

Mr. Hummerford wore glasses without sides, and had never finished shingling either his house or his store, both of which he owned. But my mother owned Mr. Hummerford, and when we left I was sure he would disappear—only to reappear when she said his name.

"A very fine man!" she said after we left. "A most unusual man from *England*." She paused to peer in her shopping bag, saw the hat, and looked away. "A very fine man but actually very peculiar," she continued. "He will never finish shingling his house, it's been that way for years." We turned the corner and her voice claimed a neighbor in an orange-red coat. "Oh, Mrs. Grever! Mrs. Grever! A sale on *beans* today. Ten cents a pound. *Green.* You must go." Mrs. Grever went.

Mr. Hummerford never did finish shingling his house, something that didn't surprise me—for what my mother's voice decreed, often happened. At its black, strident command Mr. Hummerford appeared, disappeared, my hat vanished, Mrs. Grever went off to buy beans, and my father wrote an entire book on the architecture of Italian Renaissance churches. According to my mother, he should have finished this book long before I was born, but instead spent days in the bathroom playing solitaire: Savagely, restlessly, on weekends when he wasn't teaching, my father sat on the closed lid of the toilet seat and used the laundry hamper as a table. Everyone who passed could hear the slap-slap-slap of cards on the plastic hamper. Tiring of the sound of cards, my mother would periodically scream:

"The book! the book! The goddam book! When are you going to finish the book?"

Silence would emanate from my father, an exquisite, waiting silence, the compressed silence of a desert. Soon he would emerge from the bathroom, go to his desk and begin a frightened, staccato-like typing. One felt that her voice controlled a switch in his brain, turned on some hidden interior light, a light too bright, too cold, too white for one human being to sustain. Ignited by her voice, my father wrote his book in seven years.

―――――――

Two years after my father finished his book, my mother lost her voice. By virtue of sheer volume, she had developed a polyp on one of her vocal cords and was condemned to surgery and silence. Who knew, the surgeon said, why a woman with such a quiet life would have an affliction common to circus barkers. My mother, too, drew a blank.

For six weeks, whatever my mother wanted to say would have to be conveyed through writing. To this purpose she purchased chalk and a slate. There were two virtues to this situation: First, it took her longer to write than to speak, so concision was forced upon her. Second, the house was silent.

A few days after her surgery I was summoned to the slate, where she wrote: *I do not feel comfortable using this goddam thing with anyone but my family, I will not walk around the streets like a deaf-mute. You have to come with me to Marlowe's when I return these ripped stockings.* I came with her to Marlowe's, walking through the flat streets piled with snow. My mother wrote a message about the stockings. I consulted the slate. And all the while the saleswoman looked on curiously. The ripped stockings were returned without a hitch. But on other days there were arguments: about a frozen chicken pot pie which my mother was trying to return because she claimed it had a dent in the crust; or a pair of gloves she'd purchased with lipstick stains.

"My mother says this chicken pot pie had a dent in its crust." (Me, to Mr. Hummerford.)

"Our pies are in perfect condition." (Mr. Hummerford.)

"IT HAD A DENT." (From my mother, on the slate.)

"My mother says the pie had a dent in it."

─────

These episodes were mortifying. Not only because I was twelve and pretended, with the rest of my friends, that mothers didn't exist. And not only because the mother I did have neither drove a car nor believed in God nor wore cloche hats and tiny earrings. They were mortifying because, in my own way and for my own reasons, I couldn't speak either and was terrified of being found out. It wasn't that my voice had gone, or that I couldn't think of what to say. It was that certain words wouldn't come out of my mouth, and speech was like walking through a mine-field. This had begun to happen insidiously and was getting worse like a slow and terrible plague. I never knew what words I couldn't say: one day it would be words that started with "d," another day words that started with "s." Another day it would be my name, or a country we were studying in school. I had developed a lexicon of substitutes in my head, so people couldn't guess what was going on (except when I had to introduce myself, in which case I simply declined). But now, with my mother writing things down and expecting me to repeat them, I was afraid I would be found out.

"She always *changes* what I say," my mother scribbled to my father. "She never just says what I write."

"For goddsake," said my father—weakly, as if obligated to come to my defense. "She's doing you a favor."

"Why do you always say *my mother says*?" she continued (now writing at me). "They already *know* it's me." Her nose came close, digging for an answer.

"It's just my way."

"Your *way*?" she wrote.

"Yes." I found that if I disowned whatever I was about to say it was easier to say it. But how could I tell her?

At the end of our block, in an apartment so full of ferns it looked like a rain forest, lived an elderly lady called Mrs. Dean, whose name I could never utter. Her husband had once taught Greek at Dartmouth and it was never clear why she had come to a university town in Kansas after her husband died. Mrs. Dean was thin, her face was lined like a palm, and her hands had big brown spots on them as though she had been playing with grasshoppers. Her life was considerably more orderly than my mother's, and this meant that during the time that my mother had no voice Mrs. Dean—unable to comprehend that my mother's infirmity affected her voice not her feet—would knock on the door at around five o'clock to ask if she wanted anything from the store. Whenever she knocked, my mother would make me speak for her.

"My mother says, 'hello,'" I'd always have to say. "And also that she'd like you to come in." Mrs. Dean would then stand at the threshold considering. Sometimes she would decide not to come in, and then all I had to do was give her a shopping list. But more often she would say, "Yes, I believe I will. . . ."

Our apartment stretched out like a snake from east to west. In the west was our living room and here, so they could watch the sunset, Mrs. Dean and my mother always had "tea," even though my mother drank coffee and Mrs. Dean drank sherry. I would sit near my mother on a high stool, so I could look over her shoulder and read whatever she wrote.

Mrs. Dean had a curious effect on me. In her presence, it became difficult to think of substitutes for words I couldn't say. It was as though her piercing eyes became lodged in my brain and made it almost impossible to look inside myself. For this reason, whenever Mrs. Dean visited my speech was characterized by long pauses while I pretended not to be able to read my mother's handwriting. "Cat's got her tongue, hasn't it missy?" Mrs. Dean would say, while my mother would erase the slate and begin to print. Eventually I would retrieve my secret lexicon. But I came to loathe her visits.

One day Mrs. Dean came over with an interesting piece of news. A neighbor boy named Larry Hegenberger had been operated on for appendicitis and now was in a coma at the hospital. The operation had gone without complications, and nobody had a clue as to what was wrong.

"They are *beside* themselves," said Mrs. Dean, referring to Larry's parents. "He has tubes stuck in every opening in his body. Believe me, *every* opening." While she talked, the wrinkles on her face creased and uncreased like a palm when it's being closed and opened. My mother leaned forward, and wrote, "Oh my!" on her magic slate. After I conveyed this, she then wrote: "What is the prognosis?"

"Terrible," said Mrs. Dean. "Even with all those tubes it's touch and go."

I knew Larry Hegenberger. He was good-looking in a way that made me shy, and once had stolen my eraser. It seemed horrible to me that while he was lying in the hospital, sick, with all those tubes, these two women should be talking about him as though he were a freak. The more they talked, the more the words my mother wrote became impossible to say, until finally she wrote a sentence that had nothing in it I could utter. There was no word in that sentence that didn't stick in my throat and there were no words I could think of to substitute. So all three of us sat there in silence.

"Cat got your tongue, missy?" said Mrs. Dean. And at that moment, when she looked at me, her eyes bored a hole in my head. It was a strange hole in that it penetrated the very barrier she had previously created. There were no words inside, just a series of fiery shapes. Then a single sentence rose from my throat, unbidden.

"I think it's terrible that you're talking about Larry like that, as though he's some kind of *creature.*"

My mother gasped—fighting not to speak. And Mrs. Dean looked at me through her glasses like a grasshopper. The phrase "old biddies" flew into my head, but before it came out of my mouth, I left the room.

One day after visiting the doctor, my mother came home and said: "I can talk now."

But what came form her mouth wasn't her voice: it was a croak, a sound a bird would make. Her face crumpled and she started to cry.

"My voice is *gone*," she whispered. "My voice is goddam *shot*."

With time, however, her voice returned—still a glorious instrument, able to stiffen clothes, command things from afar, announce items of interest from newspapers (her nose pointed straight into it like a diver). It was the voice of gossip, the voice of daily speech, and a voice whose capacities far exceeded my powers ("A marvelous woman!" "A stunning opera cape!")—her amazement always heralded by disbelief ("Can you imagine?" "I can't get over it," her eyes shuttering rapidly like a camera). As though a balance existed between the two of us, as my mother talked more, I talked less. Relieved of being her interpreter, I became encased in a world of silence so deep, it surrounded me like snow. And since it now turned out that there were more and more words I couldn't say, I began to find it convenient to claim that I'd lost my voice. Nobody seemed to notice or care that I had a permanent case of laryngitis. I sat peacefully in Mr. Bridge's

Latin class, relieved of having to recite the dreadful words of Caesar, letting my eyes rest on Larry Hegenberger, who had recovered from his coma and sat three seats ahead of me. Whenever I looked at him, I felt something very close to love—not just because he was handsome, but because he was my last vital link with living speech. Sometimes he would smile at me, and always, I'd smile back.

DOOR INTO DARK

"BATHS," MY MOTHER SAID. "WE MUST ALL GO TO A GOOD hotel in Lawrence and get baths with decent towels." It was early evening, and we were leaving Kansas for good. A scion of Renaissance architecture had died, and my father had been offered a job in Vermont. The movers had come and gone. My parents' friends were drinking wine in an empty apartment.

"Stay with us," a friend said. "It's too late to leave. We'll have another party."

"I can't sleep in other people's houses," my mother said. "No. Really. I can never move my bowels." Everybody laughed. "We should stop at the Willmore," she continued. "They have the nicest rooms. That lady professor from France stayed, and she loved it."

———

I went to say good-bye to my room, imagining I felt nothing. I had been having what came close to an affair with a fifty-one-year-old doctor who was supposed to help me talk, recite again in Latin class. I couldn't call him to say good-bye, and none of my friends mattered to me. I looked at my plaid wallpaper which I hated, and my mother leaned inside the door. "Are you ready?" It was clear that we were leaving.

We left Lawrence, Kansas at nine o'clock, the air still soft in early summer. There was a large round moon in the sky, a moon that didn't look real. My parents' friends gathered around the car expressing general disbelief that we were leaving at this hour. "Come take a bath at our house!" said Morla Horton, who wore long modern earrings she had baked in her own kiln. "We'll leave you alone! You can use the bathroom in peace!" My father shrugged. My mother said no. More expressions of disbelief. Kissing. Hugging. We drove through downtown Lawrence with barely a nod to the remote white, porticoed Willmore Hotel, all lit up like the moon. My mother talked on about how we would stop, take baths, relax. Nearly two hours later, when we reached the industrial steel town of Port Feyre, Kansas, she realized that we hadn't stopped at the Willmore.

"There are no vacancies," my mother announced as we drove through motels hidden in the yellow smoke of the steel mills. This was true: even though Port Feyre was a hell-hole, the *No Vacancy* signs were lit like neon samplers. "I thought we would all take baths," she said again.

My father agreed that there weren't any

vacancies. He drove to a milkshake stand, got us milkshakes, looking awkward in his baggy suit. I knew Port Feyre well from other trips east: It was the denouement of my father's no-vacancy cliff-hangers —the town where we always realized that all the motels in Kansas were filled.

"Baths," my mother said, sucking the straw of her milkshake. "*I said we should all take baths.* With towels. In a lovely hotel. I said that." My father didn't answer. The back of his neck bristled with the force of someone who intends to drive all night.

"Didn't you hear me?" my mother said.

"Yes," he said grudgingly, "I heard you."

At the outskirts of town, my father picked up speed. He drove past fiery furnaces whose smoke obscured the moon. He drove past another motel with an orange *No Vacancy* sign. My mother rummaged in her purse, looked at her face in the mirror. Then she asked:

"Who do the hell do you think I am? No, really. Who the hell do you think I am?"

Silence from my father. She answered for him: "I'm a middle-aged woman who needs my respite, that's who I am. For once we could have stopped at the Willmore and all had baths. After this lousy day. But no, not you! Drive on and on all night."

No motel was in sight. We were over the appointed edge, into the chill of being homeless. With sudden dispatch, my mother opened the door to her side of the car, and announced: "I'm getting out! I have nothing more to live for, and I'm getting out!"

My father stepped on the brake slowly, reached over to close her door. They wrestled, he lost, my mother toyed with the door like an accordion. She opened it to the frontage road—houses, steel mills, apocalyptic smoke. She closed it and Port Freyre disappeared. I said I had nothing to live for, too. My father told me to shut up.

My mother then shouted that she was really leaving and opened the door so wide I could see the whole midwest—ordinary, frightening, far too real. My father ground to the side of the road, leaned over, closed the door, then picked up speed. We drove until morning when we slept in the shelter of a truck stop. The night contained us, somehow.

COUNTRY BOY

I LEFT SOMETHING BEHIND IN KANSAS—SOMETHING dreadful, nameless, having to do with Ivan Suronovsky, the fifty-one-year-old lay analyst who had ravished me and made me happy. In Vermont, Ivan Suronovsky seemed unreal. I could barely remember his office, or the picture of his wife, or his enormous glittering glasses, or his repertoire of clichés. He was part of the flat, paralyzed midwestern landscape.

While I commenced a normal life—making friends, suddenly able to recite in class—my parents discussed Ivan in low voices. What had we really done, he and I? Who in hell did he think he was? Ivan had been my mother's analyst before he became mine and I heard her tell my father she felt guilty for taking me to see him. My father was impatient: Nothing could be done, he said. Leave it alone, for God's sake.

One night in late autumn my parents' voices rose in the living room.

"What do you know about it anyway?" my mother said. "I was the one who saw him first!"

"I know quite enough," my father answered. "Believe me. Quite enough!" This answer made me tremble because one day, as if guided by radar, I'd walked to my father's closet, reached into the pocket of a certain suit jacket, and pulled out a page from my diary: *How interesting*, I'd written, *when a fifty-one-year-old man kisses a fourteen-year-old girl for a solid fifteen minutes and licks her legs like a puppy dog. . . .*

Not wanting to hear anymore, I put on my tall rubber boots and went outside. Vermont nights weren't like nights in the midwest, where the dark was thin, equidistant, spread out against the horizon. Here the dark was dense, thick, complex, shaped by winding roads. I walked through this darkness down a road which wound all the way to the edge of town where I found a small carnival setting up. I saw crates, animals in cages, stilts that looked like crutches. Near one booth was a boy about my age with long hair tacking a roulette wheel to a piece of board. It was dark, had begun to rain, but his face loomed up at me, strangely light. *He is a country boy*, I thought, *someone different from me.*

I stood at a distance, watching him hammer. He noticed me and smiled. "Hi there," he said.

"Hi," I answered back.

Suddenly there was a sense of elevation in the air, some wild feeling of exhilaration, as though the carnival had already started. He left the booth and we fell into step. "You have to see something," he said, bringing me over to a cage. I looked inside and saw an animal who could have been a black domestic cat. "This is a panther," he said, "just a baby."

"It looks just like a cat to me," I said. He threw back his head and laughed.

In Vermont I had acquired a respectable boy-friend—a boy who excelled in math, wore black sweaters, carried an umbrella. I thought I saw him now from a distance—bemused, abstracted, looking at another booth. "Let's go for a walk," I said to the country boy.

We walked further down the road, came upon a cluster of trees and a stone bench. I looked at the country boy, we both smiled. Then we sat down on the bench and kissed—a long, full kiss, pulling us close, making me remember Ivan. In that dark, I saw Ivan's cluttered office, his desk, his armchair, his artifacts from Russia: a leather-bound book, a nesting doll in peasant clothes, a silver candlestick, a glass paper-weight. . . . Things I could touch but never bring home.

I wanted to tell the country boy about Ivan, but instead told him something that was only half-true—a story about going for a walk at two in the morning to an all-night diner, having a milkshake, meeting a

Frenchman. The walk and the milkshake were true. The Frenchman was apocryphal. The country boy listened, then kissed me again. When it was time to go he said:

"We should give each other something—a memento—for memory."

I hesitated, reached into my pocket, gave him a pencil. He reached into his pocket, handed me a photograph of the panther. "You'll see!" he said, laughing. "It isn't a cat at all!" I took the picture, fled through the beribboned night.

———

At home my mother was reading in the living room. "Where have you been?" she asked.

"To the carnival, at the edge of town."

"What did you do there?"

"Nothing. Just wandered around."

"For God's sake," she said. "Hold yourself *dear*. If you don't, nobody else will."

She came into the kitchen, began fixing herself a sandwich—brusquely, somewhat angrily. The unspoken name *Ivan* hung in the air between us. It was Russian, dark, connoting wolves, forests, ice maidens.

"It's not that I begrudge you anything," my mother continued, slapping mayonnaise onto the sandwich. "But for God's sake, you must have some sense."

I pointed out that I did have sense; since coming to Vermont I had become miraculously normal, made friends, recited in class. What else did she want from me? She shook her head.

Suddenly there was a knock on the door. It was the country boy, dripping rain. "You forgot something," he said, handing me the picture of the panther. "You dropped this when you left."

I took the picture and held it to the light. No question. It was a baby panther, not a cat. I grinned. From the kitchen my mother gave me a stern look. The look, usually reserved for magazine salesmen, meant *get him out of here.*

The country boy showed no signs of leaving. My mother stood up.

"Who are you?" she said in a low theatrical voice.

"Bill Baise, ma'am. I'm with the carnival."

My mother looked at me fiercely, pulled the skin below her left eye. Another family signal. It meant: *this person is peculiar.* "What business have you following my daughter home?" she asked.

"None, ma'am. Just wanted to give her a picture."

He didn't move from the threshold, and as all

three of us stood there together, it seemed to me that our kitchen shifted slightly, became the dark, post-World War II European kitchen that used to invade our kitchen in the midwest—flowered wallpaper, a yellow cast of light, a certain thick dimension to the furniture. My mother frowned.

"Where are you from?" she asked Bill Baise.

"Florida. Near the Everglades. I went to school in Boston, but then I quit."

"I don't believe you," said my mother. "I don't believe you at all."

When he left, disappearing down the winding road, she said to me, "Who in God's name was *that*?"

"A country boy," I answered. "He showed me around the carnival."

"For heaven's sake, don't dramatize! He was a hick."

I didn't argue. My mother returned to her sandwich. Suddenly she said: "Ivan Suronovsky. That lousy charlatan!"

I froze. She hadn't mentioned his name to me since we left Kansas. "He wasn't all that bad, Mom," I said.

"Oh yes he was. He was awful." There was a mirror in the hall, visible from the kitchen, and my mother looked into it sharply. Outside it was raining heavily; the water gushed, with sudden swells, pauses, as if the sky were opening to let more rain in. Such a pause occurred now, and the room seemed to expand. My mother hesitated, then said quietly, "You know I was seeing Ivan before you were. You *knew* that, didn't you?"

Another pause. The house began to rock, unfurling into the darkness. "Yes, Mom. I knew," I said.

"I thought he was a very sympathetic man. Very good to talk to. But then, after you started seeing him, he said to me, 'I can't see you and her at the same time. It simply isn't professional.' So what could I do? A mother's sacrifice!"

"Mom, if you *wanted* to keep on seeing him. . . ."

"No. I didn't. I got what I needed." Her voice was mildly ironic.

She didn't say what she'd needed and I didn't ask. The house swelled with the rain. I gave my mother a kiss.

"Goodnight, Mom."

"Goodnight, sweetie."

A look passed between us—neither forgiveness nor understanding, simply a meeting of the eyes. I went to my room and thought about the country boy, walking back to the carnival, through that complex darkness.

NIGHT VISIT

TWENTY-SEVEN YEARS LATER, I REMEMBERED THE DOLL I was holding as it buckled close to me, the force of my mother's eyes, my father walking me around the house, asking *Can you move your neck?* The memory came before Easter and all that spring I was afraid to be alone. I stayed with friends, then with a Jungian analyst who had a beard like Mephistopheles. "You're an introvert," he told me, "posing as an extrovert."

The Jungian analyst took me to his Westchester house, slept with me, left me there with his Jamaican maid so he could join his wife in the Bahamas. After he left, I felt I didn't have any skin: If a bannister shook, the house was falling. When the maid banged the windows, glass rattled in my throat. I left Westchester and went to England where my parents were in Oxford on sabbatical. The cobblestone streets were full of sheiks, engineering students in saris. My parents had what they called a flat.

The first night I arrived, I sat on the edge of their bed and told them I was going to die. "Nonsense," said my mother. "Go to sleep." I went to the guest room, came back, told them again I would die, and my mother said: "Get into bed with us!" I did. My mother fell asleep right away and an ineffable membrane opened between us. I felt her heart and breath, fueled by mysterious powers, love beyond her knowledge of it. My skin, in essence, returned. I went back to the tiny bedroom.

Late the next morning my mother put on a blue hat and said: "I'm going out." In a few hours she came back with a new blender and plugged it into the wall. "These things are marvelous," she said, as I watched with fragile eyes. "They'll purée almost anything." I wanted to tell her how vital and beautiful she'd seemed the night before—how her heart and breath were fueled by mysterious powers. But she began to peel peaches, still wearing her hat. "Get a knife and help," she said.

Photo: Jane Scherr

THAISA FRANK was born in the Bronx, and has lived in Manhattan, California, Illinois, France and Ohio, where she got a degree in philosophy from Oberlin College. She has also studied linguistics and philosophy at Columbia University. Her stories have been anthologized and won PEN awards, and she is the author of *Desire* (1982), a collection of short fiction. For the past fifteen years she has lived in Oakland, California, where she teaches advanced fiction writing at the University of California Extension in Berkeley and has a private practice as a psychotherapist and a writing consultant. She shares her house with her husband and her eight-year-old son.